THE FLAT TIRE

THE FLAT TIRE

FISH NEALMAN

Copyright © 2025 by Fish Nealman

All rights reserved.

No part of this publication may be reproduced, distributed, or transmitted in any form or by any means, including photocopying, recording, or other electronic or mechanical methods, without the prior written permission of the publisher/author, except in the case of brief quotations embodied in critical reviews and certain other noncommercial uses permitted by copyright law.

Publisher:
The Paper House
www.thepaperhousebooks.com

Printed in the United States of America

CONTENTS

PART I
1. Otto   3
2. Ezekiel   20
3. Linda   37
4. Martin   53

PART II
5. Hermanos   69
6. Unreasonable Times   80
7. Otto and Eli   95
8. Otto, Eli, and Linda   109
9. Camila   123
10. And, Martin   134

PART III
11. Sequoia   151
12. Miller   164
13. Teehee   179
14. Lilith   193
15. Equality   208
16. Geronimo   222
17. Daniel   234

Acknowledgments   253
About the Author   255

PART I

OTTO

CARDINAL OTTO LAMACCHIA'S ALARM CLOCK EMITTED A soft and soothing chirp, a chime chosen to cradle rather than startle. In truth, the sound was unnecessary. He'd already been up and about for almost an hour – all part of his daily routine. An alarm clock was nothing more than a humble device to serve as a contingency plan should his inner clock ever falter. However, his innate sense of time reigned supreme like everything else in his disciplined world of routine and ritual. Still, the clock provided the reassuring embrace of a reputational safety net. Cardinal Otto LaMacchia was never late.

He firmly believed arising to the wrong sounds could inadvertently provide a portal for dark social ills to enter your day. The wrong sounds, to his way of thinking, were abrasive and agitating to an awakening soul. Incessant, jarring buzzer noises probably originated from the hands of the Devil inside hell's electronics sweatshop. All signs pointed to the alarm clock being the tool of a malevolent disruptor. The same sentiment extended to the booming beats of kickdrums, Telecasters, and Roland synths should a sleep-disturbing alarm trigger a radio station.

Though lacking empirical evidence, he held firm to his opinions. He knew beliefs were sometimes driven more by faith than observable facts. In his worldview, establishing harmony between ambient sounds and a slumbering soul was paramount to embracing civility and loving one's neighbor throughout the course of the day.

As energy could influence an intention; any noise, even a sound as subtle as one's own breath, could suffice for traversing the threshold to bring one's soul back into reality. Moreover, choosing an alarm's sound represented one of the few times during his day when he could assert complete and unassailable control. This seemingly insignificant decision held profound significance in an unpredictable and chaotic world.

Otto was new to his job. It was just under three weeks since his consistory. During the evening dinner celebrating his triumphant promotion, he was careful not to overstep any boundaries. His remarks remained understated and guarded while tapping on subjects like diversity, equity, and inclusivity within secular society. Politicking in a large, open forum was an invisible force threatening to morph into a Damoclesian sword over the heads of people with future ambitions. The night unfolded, and his Chianti remained untouched. "Sober over sated" remained his mantra. He understood times were changing, and deep down, he was ready to take on the mantle of being a change agent.

He pressed the button to quiet the gentle sound and reflected for a while. An only child, and throughout his adult years, he had grown accustomed and accepting of the solace of sleeping alone. Embracing a celibate life had been a meaningful choice for him, aligning with his chosen vocation. He cherished life's blessings and always felt deep gratitude for being graced with yet another day. He'd stayed in bed for the past hour, fully awake while praying for those in need and the general condition of the planet and its inhabitants. He eased into a sitting position and then stood. He performed his morning ritual of one hundred toe touches, during which he recited the words often repeated by those in his communion: "Hail Mary, full of grace, the Lord is with thee. Blessed art thou amongst women and blessed is the fruit of thy womb… Jesus." As a sign of respect, he was always careful to insert a slight pause before intoning the name of God's son.

His bedroom exuded a quintessential sterile aesthetic influenced by post-modern minimalism. The simplicity, clean lines, and sparse use of color created an ambiance of openness and tranquility. However, the queen-sized bed was at odds with the room's overall design. Adorned with a magnificent counterpane handcrafted by Nashville's most skilled embroiderers, the fine jacquard cloth was woven in various vermilion hues intertwined with gold thread. The elaborate brocaded patterns of twisting vines danced across the sumptuous fabric. They were further complemented with lush swirls and floral motifs. The sight exuded palpable Renaissance-era opulence. No living person could behold such indulgence without marveling at the influence of the one granted the honor of possessing something so lavish for repose. The counterpane was a fitting bedtime shroud for this Prince of the Church, and it evoked the majesty of the institution's strength and endurance. If witnessed, it would be difficult to avoid noticing how unruffled the bedding appeared once he stood up – a simple testament to the quality and soundness of his slumber.

Before offering any acts professing the theological virtues of faith, hope, and love, he shaved, brushed and flossed his teeth, showered, shampooed his hair, and dressed. Part of his morning ritual was to complete *The New York Times* crossword puzzle using his iPad. Otto powered through the first seventy clues before starring at the final one: *Like a simmering stew, he could take the heat turned up from the cook's concoction without losing his savory patience.* At the same time that he exhaled through his nose, he pressed the letters "J" and "O" on the screen's keypad. The letter "B" had already been typed as part of answering sixty-nine across. Voila, the crossword was complete. He said, "I can do without the softballs, but now and again, it's nice when they throw in something theological. And, it would be nicer if English was a bit more phonetic."

Moving towards the bedroom window, Otto pulled apart the drapes. The window faced east, and Otto had a clear line of sight towards the horizon. The sky was clear. Ebbs of orange peeked in the distance. Witnessing the morning's dawn was a favorite activity to ready himself for whatever blessings the new day may bring. He loathed cloudy or rainy mornings that didn't permit the sun to announce the day with heavenly majesty. But this was not one. The orange orb lifted itself into the sky, and he said, "Blessed be God in His angels and in His saints! O God, I cannot contain the joy and delight that fills my heart. Thank you for this gift of happiness. May it inspire me to spread your love and serve your people."

Inside the cathedral, pews were filling with devoted parishioners eager for the start of the 6:30 a.m. early morning Mass. In the center of it all stood Otto – a man whose passion for God and the Church was demonstrable. The Mass began, and the air was charged with a sense of anticipation. His voice resonated throughout the hallowed space. He led the congregation in prayer, his words infused with a fervent energy captivating the hearts of those present. He exuded a deep sense of faith, an unshakable belief in the divine, that stirred the attending souls.

With each passage of scripture, Otto drew upon the virtue of faith, his eyes gleaming with conviction. This was another day when he was gifted the opportunity to relay the miracles and teachings of Jesus. His homily delved into the virtue of hope. He acknowledged the challenges and trials everyone faced in the modern world and urged trust in God's plan. He articulated a vision of a brighter future, one where love, inclusion, and compassion would conquer all. He recounted stories of kindness with a radiant smile, demonstrating the virtue that bound believers together.

Throughout the service, his exhilaration was contagious. The members of the congregation felt uplifted and inspired. Their spirits soared with a renewed sense of purpose and a closeness to the divine. An outpouring of faith, hope, and love transcended the walls and touched the heavens.

After the Mass, as the parishioners made their way outside, they uttered with awe about the transformative experience each sensed from their new cardinal. Many felt reaffirmed by their belief in God and thought they were walking on air. For Otto, leading the early morning Mass had always been more than a duty; it was a calling, an opportunity to spread theological virtues to a congregation hungry for spiritual nourishment. He bid farewell to the faithful with gratitude and humility in his heart. Then, it was his turn to be hungry.

"*Bonum mane incipit mane*," Otto said after entering the rectory.

"Please, Father, you know my conversational Latin isn't my specialty," the housekeeper said.

"My apologies, Mrs. Fitzgerald. I've just arrived from offering the early morning Mass. I meant to say, 'A good morning starts in the morning.' I hope the good Lord shines brightly upon you and yours today."

"Most certainly. I have your eggs and toast ready. Your coffee, too. Would you be caring for any juice this morning? We have orange and some fresh squeezed grapefruit," the housekeeper said with the remnants of her Irish brogue. "And less I be forgetting, the car will be here at ten to take you to the airport."

"Perfect. Thank you, and no juice this morning."

After a filling and pleasing breakfast, the Cardinal reentered his bedroom to change into his traveling attire. He donned garments far more understated than the vivid scarlet cassock and mozzetta he wore during the morning's Mass. He changed into a two-piece made-to-measure charcoal gray pinstripe suit tailored to perfection. The jacket featured smooth peak lapels and a center vent, with a single breast pocket holding a light pink linen pocket square in a presidential fold – he tended to favor light and bright colors. Affixed to the lapel, he wore a small red cross. Crisp pleated slacks broke with precision over the polished wingtip brogues in black leather. His thin dark socks disappeared under the hem of his pants. A white dress shirt provided a neutral foundation, accented by a solid, bright vermillion tie in a simple Windsor knot that acknowledged his station. Peeking out from under the sleeve of his buttoned jacket, his jeweled crucifix ring, large and ornate, was the only other indicator of his clerical status. The cufflinks were simple yet elegant mother-of-pearl ovals. In lieu of a skullcap, his silvered hair was combed and parted to frame his distinguished face. He carried himself with quiet dignity, needing no vestments to project an air of wisdom, power, and authority.

With the Vatican's decision to establish Nashville as a See, a fresh chapter in the city's spiritual journey unfurled. The newfound status required the appointment of a cardinal to lead and guide the faithful. Throughout the discernment process, Otto emerged as the prominent candidate. His compassionate demeanor captured attention.

However, his theological views deviated from the traditional beliefs held by more conservative Catholics. While he upheld the core tenets of the faith, he embraced progressive ideas, seeking inclusivity and open dialogue within the Church. This dichotomy raised questions among certain members of the clergy and the faithful, who pondered whether such diversity of thought could coexist in the hierarchy. Yet, to others, his nuanced perspective was a strength, not a liability. They recognized his ability to foster unity and collaboration, qualities that would prove invaluable in steering the Church through an expected era of change. His reputation as a team player, someone willing to bridge gaps between differing opinions, bolstered his candidacy.

During the deliberations, he remained grounded in humility. Finding solace in prayer, he sought guidance from Jesus, placing his trust in the discernment process. Finally, the momentous day arrived when the announcement came. Assuming his new position, he embraced the profound responsibility bestowed upon him. Guided by his liberal-minded approach and unwavering faith in God, he was committed to being cooperative. When Bishop LaMacchia became Cardinal LaMacchia, it marked the fruition of decades of building relationships within the Catholic Church's hierarchy. He'd prioritized establishing contacts and influence among fellow clergy members, especially those poised for advancement like himself.

As a young and adventurous missionary, he embarked on journeys far and wide, even finding himself in the Archdiocese of Ernakulam-Angamaly in Kochi, India. He was unfamiliar with the region, but wasted no time immersing himself in the local Catholic community. With genuine warmth, he forged meaningful connections with numerous priests and seminarians. An advocate for unity, he encouraged ecumenical cooperation between the Eastern and Latin rites, bridging divides and building bonds among factions seeking recognition within the Church. His natural gift for cultivating goodwill and understanding made this endeavor seem effortless. Beyond the local community, his charisma and diplomatic prowess caught the attention of Vatican officials. They admired his innate ability to network and form alliances, recognizing the potential positive impact he could have on the Church's broader mission.

In the U.S., he sought to mend rifts between progressive and conservative wings among the bishops. His razor-sharp interpersonal skills helped him latch onto common ground. He formed a diverse coalition focused on shared priorities – education, immigration, and economic justice. Through careful consultation and compromise, he got opposing factions to cooperate. He took on high-profile reconciliatory roles, reducing conflicts within and between dioceses. He became known as a mediator who could work with both liberal and traditional parishes. His reputation as a bridge builder who could work with rival factions made him an attractive candidate. The network of supporters he'd cultivated over the years lobbied, with complete discretion, on his behalf.

At 10:00 a.m. on the dot, he emerged from the rectory's front door, his luggage having departed the same way not five minutes prior. His driver, Elrod, stood by the open rear door, ready to receive him. Now in his early forties, Elrod had grown up far from the beaten track among Tennessee's rural red dirt roads. The second youngest of four boys, he learned the value of hard work and faith from his parents, who scraped by working the iron-rich fields as soybean farmers. During high school, he excelled at football, which served to earn him a scholarship to the local junior college and the hearts of the cheerleaders. After earning his associate's degree, he pursued a career in Louisville, Kentucky. Though he had little money saved up, his athletic physique and confident attitude landed him a job with an upscale transportation company. His southern charm and punctuality made him a favorite with higher-end clients, and he established a reputation as a dependable driver with an upbeat, no-nonsense professional attitude.

He loved staying active in the gym during his spare time, where he maintained his muscular frame. His devotion to weight training started as a high school freshman and remained a lifelong hobby. At twenty-seven, he entered and won a statewide amateur bodybuilding competition.

After a few years, he was hired as a private driver for the prestigious Archdiocese of Louisville. Taking immense pride and satisfaction in his role, he chauffeured the archbishop and other revered clergy to their various masses, conferences, and meetings. He'd grown up in the Catholic faith, so he cherished the opportunity to serve and support, feeling a deep sense of fulfillment in contributing to his faith in a meaningful capacity.

Being aware of Elrod's work ethic and discretion, Cardinal LaMacchia selected him as his driver. The role required constant readiness for travel and long hours, but Elrod didn't mind. Though he never carried a weapon, Elrod was quick to associate himself with Otto's security detail. His blend of brawn and gentility was suited to deter threats with utmost grace. His toned arms and heroic-jawed physique seemed at odds with his genuine humility. Steadfast and true to his nature, he remained the nice southern boy his parents raised.

"Good morning, Elrod," Otto said.

"Your Excellency, how are we today?"

"Excellent, most excellent, Elrod. A beautiful morning."

Otto entered the sizeable black SUV through the open rear passenger door. Elrod closed the door and walked behind the vehicle to the driver's side door. Sitting behind the leather-wrapped wheel, he buckled his seatbelt. Pushing the polished stainless 'go' button, the supercharged big block roared into life.

"CNN, please," Otto said.

Elrod tuned the vehicle's satellite radio to the requested news station. Moments later, both occupants heard, "This is CNN's weather anchor and severe weather expert based in the network's world headquarters in downtown Atlanta. Meteorologists like myself mark September tenth as the statistical peak of hurricane season, an unofficial meteorologist holiday, and right on cue, Geronimo's eye made landfall a few moments ago just east of Galveston. We haven't seen any signs that this Category Four hurricane is losing force. It's still pushing wind speeds close to the magic one hundred and fifty-five miles per hour mark. That would place it into Category Five territory. We've already reported that this year's hurricane season got off to a rapid start and is showing no signs of slowing down. As many of our listeners already know, we're on our second run through the naming alphabet, and there's yet another tropical depression forming off the west coast of Africa. In the last segment, we heard from Doreen that record hot ocean temperatures in the Atlantic allowed storms to form early in the deep tropics."

For the moment, Nashville's skies were clear, and the late summer sun beat over the city with pleasantry. Otto's phone dinged.

"One moment, Elrod."

"Yes, Excellency." Elrod muted the radio.

"I've just received a text message from the airline. They're canceling my flight because my aircraft was arriving from Austin. The federal authorities have shut down all airports within two hundred and fifty miles of the Gulf Coast. Ooh, here's another. This one says I won't be notified until later this afternoon about my rebooking. Geronimo is causing a logistical nightmare."

Without skipping a beat, Elrod said, "Let me drive you, sir."

"What?"

"D.C.'s probably not more than seven hundred miles, and I should still be able to get you there in time for dinner."

"Elrod!"

"It's no problem at all."

"Most kind. I've always said that you were a godsend and a saint. Thank you, Elrod."

Elrod navigated the mid-morning traffic; Otto completed the Wordle puzzle in two tries but failed to guess the Connections challenge in the requisite six. He started working on the crossword from *The Boston Globe*. With one hand on the wheel, Elrod made a minor adjustment to the rearview mirror and straightened his black tie before merging onto the eastbound lane of I-40.

The first few hours passed without noticeable impediment, aside from Otto grumbling about an eleven-letter word for "Damask bedding fit for a Medici." After having tried "brocade," "bedspread," "eiderdown," and even "craquelure," he dug deep and dredged up "counterpane." Around the three-hour mark, the first of the journey's snafus presented itself. They were between Knoxville and Morristown, having maintained a steady cruising speed of a couple of miles per hour over the posted limit. The first situation turned out to be less of a snarl and more of a DeWalt demolition screwdriver with a solid steel core for bend resistance, which had tumbled off the back of a passing late-model long-bed Chevy pickup straight into their path.

Elrod felt a jolt ricochet through his hands as the front

passenger side tire shredded itself on the implement. While he wrestled with the steering wheel, Otto muttered, "My Lord, good heavens!" and made the sign of the cross with haste. Coming to a stop on the shoulder, Elrod stepped out of the SUV and frowned at the flaccid mass of rubber, once a tire in its former life. Otto alighted. Watched Elrod strip off his jacket and tie, and offered a blessing for the successful changing of wheels. Within twenty minutes, the vehicle was back on the highway and cruising at its prior speed. Elrod took the off-ramp for I-81 and began offering a slew of Hail Marys for smooth sailing when a pebble ricocheted off the windshield with uncanny precision. What started as a pockmark spiderwebbed into a multitude of vision-obscuring cracks over the next fifty miles. They were close to Bristol, a town bisected by the Tennessee-Virginia border. At an Interstate rest stop, Elrod called the local Safelite AutoGlass franchise on Volunteer Parkway for emergency windshield repair service. Otto contacted St. Anne's on Euclid for a bottle of holy water. "Just in case," he said.

Once more, they were back on the road, but it didn't take long for the engine to start sputtering. Elrod's brow creased with concern. *What the Devil*, he thought. The fuel gauge showed half-full, but the car gasped like the last twenty-pound rainbow trout he'd landed at Old Man Nelson's place on South Holston Creek. A desperate battery of prayers from the backseat confirmed they were now well and truly stuck. With no cell service on the desolate stretch of highway, Elrod left Otto to wait in the comfort of the

THE FLAT TIRE

rear seat as he headed out to scout for signs of civilization. Shortly thereafter, he came across a run-down garage and noticed a dilapidated Airstream trailer and a hand-painted sign that read, "Appalachian Auto and Cycle Repairs."

The garage was owned by a good ol' boy named Bubba, a shirtless, overall-clad septuagenarian who eyed Elrod with suspicion. "Been a while since a suited man came 'round here," Bubba said.

Not more than another hour passed before the SUV was brought back to Bubba's and raised on a creaking garage lift. Bubba worked and prattled on about his late wife, Bobbie, and her famous blackberry and rhubarb pie. He offered Otto and Elrod a slice of his take on her recipe. Elrod nodded in his typical polite manner while Otto engaged with the lonely man about his life's story.

By the time the fuel pump was replaced, the evening air was in full flight, and the pair were *on the road again*. Elrod hummed a few bars to himself.

He's no Willie Nelson, Otto thought, followed immediately by, *Bless me, Lord, for I have sinned. It's not the man's fault that You did not gift him with musical talent.*

D.C. was still four hours ahead, but Elrod saw increasing signs of life and began to breathe a little easier. A ghastly new grinding sound erupted from the engine. He pulled over just before the engine compartment belched a mass of steam into the starlit night. Lifting the hood revealed a mangled mess of shrapnel.

Resigned yet determined, Elrod made sure the Cardinal was secure, then began walking by himself towards a flickering light. He encountered a rural bar near Christiansburg, a dim and dusty affair decorated with dust-covered deer antlers and multiple animals living on the walls in a taxidermy-ed state. Elrod approached the bar and asked the barman which patron owned the Jerr-Dan heavy-duty carrier parked outside. After landing on an agreeable financial arrangement, the Jerr-Dan owner drove Elrod back to the crippled SUV, loaded it onto the flatbed, and placed Elrod and Otto into the back seat of his cab for the journey's remaining four hours.

"Buckle up," the owner said.

"Well, Elrod, it appears Our Lord has seen fit to test us today."

Elrod began to concur until he noticed a whimsical twinkle in the Cardinal's eye.

"But as much as chance may dictate our path, it's our choice to see each unexpected turn as an opportunity that determines where we arrive. I dare say that each of our breakdowns gave more than they took. The stalled moments and periods of wait granted time for conversation, compassion, and even a slice of homemade pie we otherwise would have missed," Otto said.

Elrod nodded, a smile forming. "Why yes, Your Eminence. I do believe you've found enlightenment in the unpredictability of it all."

"Indeed, Elrod, for is not faith tested strongest when the way is most unclear? I can say my resolve feels fortified after our exploits today. While at my meeting tomorrow, why don't you trade in our wreck for something more likely to get us back home? The See can wire the funds."

Delayed by happenstance, Otto arrived at his hotel at 2:00 a.m., which was still sufficient time for a short nap. Elrod had his own room.

Summing up their day, Otto said, "Remember, intention matters more than distance, and a journey more than a destination. Such are the mysteries of the road, my dear Elrod. Sleep well."

EZEKIEL

RABBI EZEKIEL RAHABI STEPPED ONTO THE *BIMAH* AND GAZED at his small, intimate congregation. Truth be told, he didn't even have a *minyan*, a mandated quorum of adults. In Judaism, prayer is considered a communal act, and according to Talmudic law, specific prayers and rituals require a certain number of people. A decade ago, he had stood before much larger crowds, pitching to eager young quants on the latest market trends and profits to be made. But now, as rabbi of this quiet New Jersey town, he spoke on ancient wisdom, not wealth.

Without a *minyan* and not wanting to falsify his accounting, he chose to forgo the *bar'chu* and *kaddish* from his litany. He began his sermon with a pronounced smile. He loved this modest house of worship. Though his path here was unexpected, his heart filled with purpose.

Ezekiel worked to make Judaism feel accessible and relevant. He shied away from overt preaching, opting for entertaining parables with meaning. In one memorable sermon, the story of Jonah and the whale was related to a New York Jets fan "getting swallowed up" in an obsession with their team. Laughs would always yield to moments of poignant reflection.

Drawing upon his secular past, he made scripture resonate in surprising ways. He knew the five books of Moses contained timeless lessons that could serve his congregation well if only brought into a modern context. Although honor and integrity were concepts at odds with his past work on Wall Street, their intrinsic meanings mattered in his small synagogue.

He was gentle and thoughtful when counseling congregation members through difficulties. His experiences gave him a pathway for understanding and empathy. When a teenager confided in him about her depression, he used King David's Psalms as a means to find light in the darkness. In comforting a grieving widower, he recounted Jacob wrestling the angel to encourage grappling with the mysteries of loss.

An older teenage boy told him that God now felt distant and impersonal. He went on to say, "I'm probably better suited to becoming an agnostic." Ezekiel told him that he understood how he felt and engaged the boy in a dialogue to see if he could help him view God in a different light.

"I appreciate how becoming an agnostic might help you hedge your bets. But you'll also remove all your options to pray for the Jets to make it into the playoffs this year."

"Based on my experience, I don't think he listens," the boy said.

"I'm sure he listens," Ezekiel said. "But you have to remember there are thousands of young men just like yourself, all making the exact same prayer for their team. Maybe God tries to give everyone a turn every now and again – you are young, but surely you've heard the legend of Joe Namath? After all, God can't have every team win the Super Bowl every year. It's unfortunate, but God can't always make everyone happy with every prayer. On the other hand, God gave us free will, so we have to try to make things work out. This is a gift God gave us – we can use it any time we want to. In fact, when we put our own energy into making something happen, we get to feel a sense of accomplishment. It would become very mundane if everything were handed to us whenever we offered a prayer. Think about it: If all your prayers were answered as you hoped, you could end up taking the life out of living!"

"I suppose. But none of that is helping make God feel any closer."

"Okay. Let me ask you, have you ever considered the meaning behind the prayer we try to say every day?"

The boy gave a beguiled look.

"The *Shema*," the Rabbi said.

"No."

"How does the *Shema* start?"

"*Shema Yisrael*, which means 'Hear O Israel,'" the boy replied.

"And, what do you think that might mean?"

"Something about a country that hears? Honestly, I thought it was a little dumb and didn't really mean anything useful."

Ezekiel smiled and laughed in an attempt to continue breaking down the barriers. "Let's see if we can't make heads and tails of what it might mean."

"Okay."

"What do you think the word *Shema* might mean?"

"Hear."

"Do you think that it could mean anything else?"

"I don't know."

"It can also mean listen. When used in this particular prayer, it's a word that becomes an imperative command. It's urging us to pay attention and heed what is about to be said. A modern translation might be, 'Hey, bro! Check it out, I've got some real cool stuff to drop on you, you dig?'"

The two laughed at Ezekiel's lame attempt to sound young and hip.

"You're about fifty years behind on your *groovy* lingo," the boy said.

Ezekiel nodded and continued. "So, *Shema* can have several uses that involve hearing, understanding, obeying, and proclaiming. Agreed?"

The boy's mouth twitched in agreement.

"Now. What does 'O' mean?"

"Of. Like four o'clock? But why isn't there an 'O' in the Hebrew version?"

"The translation is helping to give us a little clue. Let me see! Do you know Sinead O'Connor, she was a pop star, or the famous painter Georgia O'Keeffe? Or, do you have any friends in school whose last name starts with 'O' apostrophe?"

"There's someone in my math class – Robbie O'Brien."

"Good, good. The 'O' apostrophe is symbolic of being a descendant. O'Brien refers to a descendant of Brien. The Scottish use 'Mac' to mean the same thing. Muslims use *'Bin.'* And in Hebrew, we use *'Ben'* when the first name is for a boy and *'Bat'* when the first name is for a girl. The Dutch use *'Van der,'* and the Spanish will use *'de la.'* Are you with me so far?"

A nod.

"Now, 'Israel' was the name given to Jacob after he wrestled with an angel and became a symbol of the spiritual legacy he would pass on to future generations. The fascinating thing about the word Israel can't be garnered from English letters. We have to use the Hebrew. The Hebrew pronunciation, Yisrael, is made up of five Hebrew letters. Can you tell me what they are?"

"*Yod, shin, resh, alef,* and *lamed.*"

"Excellent. Now, who are regarded as the patriarchs and matriarchs of Israel?"

"Abraham, Isaac, Jacob, Sarah, Rebecca, Rachel, and Leah."

"And, if we use the Hebrew spellings, what is the first letter for each name?"

"Abraham is *alef.* Isaac and Jacob are both *yod.* Sarah is *shin.* Rebecca and Rachel are both *resh.* And, Leah would be *lamed.*"

"Perfect. Now, if we take each unique letter from their names, we get *yod, shin, resh, alef,* and *lamed.* In other words, Yisrael is an acronym for our forefathers and foremothers. How cool is that?"

The boy smiled.

"If we now view the start of the *Shema* as 'Hear, O Israel to mean 'Hey, bro! Check it out. I've got some real cool stuff to drop on you, you dig? Now hear this: You are the descendant of Abraham, Isaac, Jacob, Sarah, Rebecca, Rachel, and Leah.' It's how the Torah refers to you and just you. It's how God put your personal name into the Torah. The next part of the prayer says, 'The Lord is our God, and the Lord is one.' So, the *Shema* is a personal prayer connecting you through the legacy of our ancestors – from your parents to your grandparents, to your great-grandparents, and all of the way back to Abraham and Sarah – where everyone is letting you know this is the guy with whom you can have a personal experience, from you to him and him to you. This personal relationship is powerful; it's why we cover our eyes when we start this prayer. Take this as a start to finding your faith, trust, and love in having a personal relationship with God. Can you try that? Because he's talking directly to you, and no one else, in this prayer."

The nod was more enthusiastic this time – all Ezekiel needed.

Providing guidance such as this filled him with a

profound sense of reward, not in terms of accolades or wealth but one that helped ease the lingering guilt and shame he carried. It was an ongoing process, and with each passing day, internal peace grew.

Adding the ByteSize streaming service as a social outlet, his sermons reached audiences hungry for meaning. ByteSize provided snappy bite-sized digestibles – the brand's euphemism for short videos that would sometimes be referred to as an "edible." He was humbled to think that his words resonated with people across mountain ranges and oceans. The influence felt real when people shared their own stories of growth with emails or their own uploaded digestibles. His lighthearted videos unpacking the Torah made Judaism accessible and relatable to millions seeking guidance. Comments flooded in from inspired subscribers who saw their faith in a new light thanks to the shared insights.

After watching his videos, one message came from a young banker who reported fraud at his firm rather than partake. Others wrote of strengthening their faith, overcoming adversity, and finding community. His teachings bettered lives and validated his work more than his hollow fiscal success ever did.

Nevertheless, Ezekiel's favorite aspect was shepherding his small congregation, not the viral online fame. He cherished celebrating weddings, *bat* and *bar mitzvahs*, mourning with grief-stricken families, and watching babies blessed during Shabbat services.

By taking the time to know each congregant's story

through joy and sorrow, he forged lasting bonds of family. The community blessed him with an enriching sense of belonging he never knew could exist. No longer did he dwell on past regrets. He was filled with gratitude for the purpose that sustained him. Ezekiel concluded his sermon on the *bimah*, smiling once more at the faces before him. This humble house of worship had become his home.

At Tufts, Ezekiel thought he had it all. He finished top of his class in both his undergraduate and graduate degrees and then landed a coveted position at a prestigious Wall Street firm. His pride took possession of a lavish, high-rise condominium on William Street. The building and his apartment had been designed by the British-Ghanaian architect, Sir David Adjaye, whose work weaved disparate elements of inspiration from culture to technology and science. Like all of the tenants, Ezekiel chose to overlook the vibrations from the subway trains rolling under the building in favor of the panache of the address.

Ezekiel's meteoric success trading securities was matched only by his voracious appetite for the lifestyle it afforded him. But underneath the bespoke Madison Avenue suits and bravado, he held an inkling that something was missing. Over time, the greed and corruption poisoning the industry got under his skin and took its toll. After years of living in a hyper-competitive, status-seeking culture that pushed mortals into prioritizing profits and prestige over ethics, Ezekiel was the bullseye in an insider trading scandal.

Although embarrassed about his past, he never hid his

story from the remote Jewish community nestled in Sussex County. In this quiet town, far from the temptations and trappings of his old life, Ezekiel flourished. He combined the pragmatism and insight gleaned from his secular experiences with his passion for Judaism. Studying Torah now brought true fulfillment. He delighted in mining layers of meaning from subtle nuances in the theological text.

Over time, wounds healed, and a sense of peace swaddled his soul. The glittering lure of wealth and prestige that once burned white hot left him fizzled, empty, and alone. Now, Ezekiel walked a different path, slower and more straightforward but rich in meaning. He found his purpose by uncovering the lessons in the Torah and from his own mistakes. What he sought was not in skyscrapers or stock prices but in the timeless wisdom that guided each step along life's journey.

When Ezekiel decided to follow a different path and dive into Torah and Talmud studies, he was often distracted. Through it all, he stuck with it and began to gain a deeper appreciation for the ancient texts. He discovered new meaning in stories he had breezed through as a youth while attending his local *cheder*, a school that taught the basics of Judaism and the Hebrew language. He took copious detailed notes on resonated interpretations and compiled a manuscript of teachings.

He leaned on his faith to maintain hope and retain a strong sense of purpose. He tuned out cynicism and focused on self-improvement. The hours turned into days, days into months, and months into years. He made studying a ritual to nourish his mind and spirit.

Though Ezekiel had achieved more career success than he dared dream on Wall Street, under the surface, he came to realize the wealth, prestige, and perverse meaning of life attached to an all-consuming career was unsatisfying. He reflected on the values his orthodox parents had tried to instill in him growing up. Community, spirituality, and wisdom – not wealth – brought intrinsic rewards. He was determined to realign his life toward those principles.

Ezekiel brought an unconventional background to his role as rabbi. His past was atypical. With his unique history, he connected Torah teachings to contemporary dilemmas. He used anecdotes and metaphors from sports or pop culture to explain complex theological concepts. He wanted to make the lessons feel relevant, not abstract or obscure. He always spoke with a candid, non-judgmental style, more interested in enlightening than condemning. He often related the biblical rivalry between Joseph and his brothers to the competitive dynamics of siblings in a rock band. He likened Jacob's wrestling with the angel to a boxer battling his inner demons before a big match, someone who also needed to fight for growth and self-awareness to become a real champion.

Ezekiel was open about sharing his mistakes, hoping they could help guide others. By reflecting on his crimes and rehabilitation, he tried to provide a moral compass oriented towards the real world, not lofty ideals. His teachings acknowledged human flaws while showing pathways to redemption.

In one of his popular digestibles, he told the Talmudic story of Honi. "Honi saw an old man planting a carob tree. So, Honi asked him, 'This tree takes seventy years to bear fruit. Do you expect to live long enough to enjoy it?' The man replied that he found the tree in bloom when he was born, and his ancestors had planted it for him. So, too, will he plant for those who come after."

After a brief pause in his storytelling, he continued. "The patience and selflessness of this man resonates across generations. It's so easy in our fast-paced world to focus only on the present, chasing after whatever brings us instant satisfaction. But there is honor and purpose in building something that may outlast us, even if we don't get to reap its benefits. Our society values those who align with quarterly earnings reports, quick fortunes, and celebrities who can draw viral attention. Yet real wisdom often lies in slow, steady nurturing. Like the man planting the carob tree, we find fulfillment in leaving a legacy for the future. What seeds could each of us plant, not for ourselves, but for those who will one day take our place? What matters is continuing the chain, knowing we are one small and meaningful link."

Through insights like this, he tried to share timeless lessons in a meaningful way for modern audiences.

Ezekiel became fascinated by the intricate workings of language. During the sermon at his *bar mitzvah*, the Rabbi told a story. "A young Jewish boy lived in Lithuania, in the

THE FLAT TIRE

city of Kretinga. The city lies about ten miles inland from the Baltic Sea. The summers are mild, and the temperature seldom goes above seventy. Nobody has to worry about getting sunburned! In contrast, the winters are harsh, and the temperature seldom goes above freezing. Frostbite is a different story! One you have to worry about. Spring came, and the ponds thawed, but the water remained cold. On his way home from school one day, he decided to take a shortcut because he'd left school a little late. Walking past Kretinga Park Pond, he got too close to the edge, slipped, and fell into the water. Struggling to get back to the bank, he saw two Russian soldiers walking by. 'Help me. Help me,' he cried. The soldiers looked at the struggling Jewish boy, laughed, and continued to walk on by. The boy grew weaker. He saw two other Russian soldiers. This time, he shouted, '*Mochkrushys. Mochkrushys.*'"

The Rabbi took a moment to look at the congregation, not the *bar mitzvah* boy, and said, "Please pardon my French!" *It's not often that you get to throw in motherfucker into a sermon in a meaningful way,* he thought.

"The soldiers got annoyed by being called *Mochkrushys*. They said to the boy, 'How dare you! You can't talk to us that way.' They stopped, pulled him out of the water, and punched him in the face. They left him lying on the ground with a bleeding nose and a black eye. Although the boy was injured, he lived and didn't drown. Sometimes, your choice of words can be the difference between life and death. Always remember: your words matter."

Ezekiel laughed. He thought the story was funny but

failed to grasp the true meaning of the parable until years later. When the message resonated, it spurred his fascination with the intricate workings of language. He started to delight in vocabulary quizzes and spelling bees and collected new words like treasures. While in the cutthroat finance world, his linguistic passions got pushed aside, but his love of etymology returned. He studied the Torah and word origins and how meanings shifted across centuries and cultures.

Intrigued by how subtle changes in terminology reflected societal values and attitudes, he delved into how other languages influenced languages. While the current use of "Pardon my French" means to apologize for using profane or offensive language, that wasn't always the case. When William the Conqueror invaded England in 1066, he brought with him the French language. French was seen as a fancier language, and everyday words were flipped into terms of prestige. House became mansion, pig became pork, and offspring became progeny. Allowance, literature, purify, sentiment, and even the idiom *c'est la vie* all got thrown in for good measure. The British soon began, in a literal way, to highlight their use of French, "Pardon my French." By the mid-eighteenth century, the phrase morphed into its present-day excuse for using salty speech.

The evolution of language came to mirror humanity's constant grappling with moral complexities in Ezekiel's eyes. He discovered new profundity in the Torah by examining the original Hebrew text. He researched contexts and interpretations of key terms to unpack layers of nuance. He loved exploring how certain concepts like righteousness and sin took on new dimensions over generations.

In one study session, he traced the phrase "fear not" as it was used throughout the Torah. In ancient times, this often implied showing reverence to God. But by the Rabbinic era, fear not also came to mean having faith in one's convictions. Inspiration was found in both meanings – respect and courage. In another instance, he examined the Hebrew word for charity, *tzedakah*. Its root meaning was tied to justice and fairness. Giving *tzedakah* was not mere generosity but an act of righteousness to the sages. The etymology revealed why Jewish tradition compels compassion for those in need.

Ezekiel followed the evolution of colloquial terms, like the changing connotations of "wicked" from evil to awesome. He chuckled, seeing how slang semantic drifts reflected generational values and cultures.

When counseling congregants, Ezekiel paid close attention to the words they used, helping uncover deeper emotions and struggles. He grasped the power of language to provide solace, express truths, and steer toward moral purpose. But most fulfilling was when he witnessed the impact of his own words. Congregants told him his insights "spoke" to them. His linguistic approach to the Torah shed new light on their faith and lives.

By never taking words for granted, he discovered profound complexity and meaning. He saw language not as static symbols but as evolving, breathing entities connecting humanity across time and spiritual traditions. This enriched his journey, one word at a time.

The journey he now faced was a five-hour drive to Washington, D.C. The dawn's early light was in full force when Ezekiel loaded up his jalopy, a twenty-something-year-old faded blue Honda Civic with its fair share of scratches and dings. Although he could have flown, dealing with Newark Airport never thrilled him for short flights. Mile after mile, he traversed the uneventful terrain of New Jersey's I-95. While the car gave everything it could, every other vehicle seemed to be going faster. His mind wandered, reminiscing about childhood vacations while his tires glided smoothly over the asphalt. The scenery passed by in a blur, with billboards advertising the wonders of the Garden State and the occasional tree lining the side of the road.

He began to notice an unusual pattern of cars pulled over to the side of the road, one after the other, all with their hazards flashing. He drove by the first car and saw the driver, a middle-aged man in a worn-out plaid shirt, kneeling beside the left front tire with a jack in hand. Ezekiel offered a sympathetic smile and a wave as he passed by, making a mental note to be on the lookout for any perilous Jersey debris. It wasn't long before he saw a second, this time, a small SUV. Even from a distance, he could make out the stout younger woman's grease and dirt-smeared hands. She was tightening the lug nuts. A sense of *déjà vu* washed over him.

By the time he saw the third car, he felt like there was a

contagious tire epidemic spreading along the southbound lane of the interstate. He kept a keen eye on the road, looking for any signs of nails, glass, or other rubble to explain the bizarre phenomenon. However, the road appeared pristine, leaving him puzzled as to what could be causing so many flat tires in such a short span.

With every passing car, he became more intrigued and concerned. *Am I waiting for my turn?* he thought and intentionally reduced his speed.

Once he'd crossed into Delaware, he stopped seeing vehicles along the side of the road. He resumed a faster cruising speed, and by the time he reached Maryland, the landscape had become urbanized. He felt his feelings returning to a state of normalcy. Smiling to himself, he sensed the gravity and history of America and all those who had traveled this route even before there were cars. He approached the famed capital beltway, the sixty-four miles of concrete and asphalt encircling his destination. Inching along in the perpetual heavy traffic, he held no frustration. Instead, he gazed out in awe at the iconic scenery coming into view.

He passed the towering white pillars of Arlington Memorial Bridge, conjuring images of solemn funeral processions for the nation's fallen heroes. He saw the epic monuments of the National Mall, stoic amid the hustle and bustle of this metropolitan city. He peered up at the obelisk form of the Washington Monument. He recalled Dr. King's famous speech echoing from the Mall's hallowed ground. The U.S. Capitol dome appeared statuesque, and he said a quiet prayer for wisdom and justice to prevail in those chambers. Driving past the Smithsonian's red brick façade, he could see the sign for his hotel.

By mid-afternoon, he had parked his car and checked into the hotel. Finding he had time to kill, there would be plenty of time to eat and attend the *Ma'ariv* – evening service – at Kesher Israel in Georgetown.

LINDA

DOCTOR LINDA HERZOG, THE RENOWNED AMERICAN philosopher and gender theorist, received the first of her two doctorates from Cambridge as an international exchange student. Her second was gained from Berkley. Within erudite circles, she was known for her work on the critique of identity politics, the politics of resistance, and the performativity of gender. Herzog explained in the respected quarterly journal, *The Philosophical Review*, that an act can be considered "performative" if the action produces a series of effects. Applying the concept to gender, she argued that gender is performative because there can be no gender identity until an act is classified. She has further claimed, "Actions are continuously constituting identity." In layperson terms, she suggested gender is not something we are but something we do.

Her groundbreaking research on gender performativity had a profound impact on feminist theory, queer theory, and critical theory. By questioning the conventional belief of gender as rigid and inherent, she became a staunch advocate for breaking free from the confines of traditional gender norms to embrace a more fluid and open understanding of expression. Her work opened possibilities for exploring diverse ways of being and expressing one's gender identity.

In a recent lecture, a student with an apparent androgynous appearance raised their hand to pose a question.

"And, what are your preferred pronouns?" the student asked.

"Let me start by saying that a preference is liking a cabernet sauvignon more than a chardonnay, enjoying a cozy mystery novel over a thriller, or McDonald's over Burger King. But pronouns? For most people, pronouns are not a matter of preference but a statement of fact. That aside, we are seeing a preoccupation with pronouns. I believe the fixation is distracting us from the deeper and more important conversations we need about gender identity and the challenges many in today's society still face."

"I don't disagree, but what pronouns do you use?"

"Doctor," Linda said.

"That's your title, not your pronoun."

"Doctor," she replied with a take-or-leave-it tone.

A follow-up question on the same topic was asked by another student clad in something resembling a goth Halloween costume.

THE FLAT TIRE

Linda replied, "You're losing the narrative. You're shifting the conversation to one of perceived political correctness, grammar, and linguistics rather than one intrinsic to the human experience and the journey behind each individual identity."

As the first daughter born into a Jewish-Italian family in Bridgeport, Connecticut, she was encouraged to bury herself in her studies. In retelling her youth, she would use the word "mandated" to describe the type of encouragement she received. Both parents were judges – resolute, principled, and progressive conservatives who believed in upholding the rule of law. At home, they could be both judge and jury. Their no-nonsense approach and commitment to discipline shaped the family's values and infused a deep sense of responsibility. Their parenting style was capped off by raising the three children to follow in their intellectual interests. Her parents were politically active, and even before she could walk or understand language, Linda was exposed to a variety of political and social issues. The constant onslaught of verbal bickering about what people were doing wrong in their lives had an overwhelming impact on her. It steered her interests toward the fields of philosophy and critical theory.

In her book, *Enough Already*, a critique of Zionism, she wrote about her Jewish heritage and how it shaped her thinking. In one passage, she noted: "My family's Jewishness was less about its religious affiliation and more about how one could successfully carry a stigma in the world." Overall, she felt her family's identity was shaped by a commitment to social justice and by offering a critique of those who ignored innate human complexities.

No doubt, her family background had an intense impact on her work as a philosopher. Even in high school, she was known to argue how identities were something, "Not fixed or essential, but constantly being negotiated and performed." More than anything, she wanted to challenge any dominant power structure to create a more just and equitable world. Some considered her one of the most influential philosophers of any recorded generation. In some smaller circles, she was regarded as a "royal pain in the butt and someone who enjoys seeking out an eternal golden braid of controversy."

She received her undergraduate degree from Yale and her graduate degree from NYU. After completing both of her doctorates, she taught at several universities, including Wesleyan, Johns Hopkins, and the University of California, Berkeley. For the past five years, she'd occupied the Professor of Rhetoric and Comparative Literature chair at Princeton.

Not What You Think was the title of her first postgraduate book, and it focused on the mutable nature of gender assignment. Gender was something "relentlessly negotiated and renegotiated," she wrote. In her follow-up masterpiece, *Weaponized Words*, she postulated, "Speech is always open to resignification." Her lesser-read tome was entitled *Fragility*. "In order create a fair and equitable world, every individual is burdened to live with and through precarity," she wrote.

Primarily out of gross misunderstanding, *People*

Magazine summed up her works as having the potential to reach an audience size that could be counted on one hand. Linda didn't care. Her royalty checks demonstrated the "hand" *People Magazine* referenced exhibited over six hundred thousand fingers.

True to her nature, she did nothing to shy away from controversy. Her numerous critics accused her of undermining the very category of gender and "promoting radical relativism." In contrast, her allies argued her work was essential for "understanding the complexities of being human." By her early thirties, she'd developed a rather tricky habit of not paying attention to either side. Her mother explained it as a "family-learned skill to ignore the people who doubt us." Especially in the early period of her career, she was sufficiently arrogant to think that her ideas were beyond the grasp of most. She viewed her primary purpose as "challenging the status quo and formulating new possibilities for social justice."

Her autobiography, *Frontiersman*, received critical acclaim, but the sales were lackluster even though the audiobook version performed better than expected. Social media got hold of a story that one of the chapters was not included in the final publication. Why the book's editor, or whomever was in charge at the time, chose to drop the chapter remained a mystery. In the popular blog post curated by @transitioned, the missing narrative was called "gobbledygook, suffering from a tangled web of thoughts without coherence." Still, a hyperlink was shared to where a fragment of the work was nestled. The webpage mentioned that everything had been, "Salvaged from an abandoned unencrypted hard drive." Shortly after, the webpage disappeared, but the Internet never forgets:

> *The evening rises, and the darkness looms, threatening to swallow everything in its path. But there's a silver crescent moon hanging above, casting its ethereal glow, and among the rustling of trees, a faint call reaches my ears. It's barely audible, a mere whisper, yet it resonates deep within my heart, and its pulsating urgency feels like a shout.*
>
> *My parents' faint, remanent voices echo in my mind, beckoning me to follow. I stand in the midst of a maze, both real and metaphorical, trying to untangle the labyrinth built inside my head. Another voice asks me to confront my inner demons. So, I did. I thought I slayed the beast, laying it to rest. Yet, I find myself still entangled in my own thoughts, seeking a way out. I might have navigated this darkness more easily, but here I am, lost. Uncertain if what I heard was truly just me or a door closing. Finally, shedding preconceived ideologies hatched from parental mumblings during childhood.*
>
> *I assure myself, then try to muster the strength to push through the maze, wishing I had possessed the foresight to lay a guiding thread. The darkness, ever-present, envelopes me and leaves me blind to the path ahead. Roaming through the sacred groves while bathing in the moon's gentle light, I know I need to seek solace. The weight of the sword I tether feels so heavy. I have to let it go while feeling defenseless in this empty place. It's funny how vulnerability seeps in when no one's watching.*
>
> *I had been blind in thinking that I needed someone,*

expecting to be tied down. Instead, I was given a map to navigate my emotions. If only I had known, I could have listened from the very start. I look at my watch and recognize it's midnight somewhere. Outside, I hear soft dripping water against the adjacent inhospitable wall, magnified in this desolate lab on this desolate campus. It's more a feeling than a substance, but substantial enough to make me feel like I'm drowning in my own thoughts. I admit my weakness, so now it's time to move on. I need to find comfort and strength in facing my own free will and traverse the labyrinth of my complications to untangle this maze.

She was a complex person, and her ideologies ran deep. She possessed a unique ability to navigate between political economies of power and the cultural politics of identity. Balancing materialism and poststructuralism never posed a challenge as long as it encouraged, from her perspective, "critical thinking about life." Her remarkable ability to integrate differing viewpoints allowed her to shed light on important issues and inspire others to reflect on our society.

The concept that our behavior can be predicted based on the inner workings of our biological makeup can be traced back to the seventeenth-century French philosopher, Descartes. He believed in dualism. He held there was a separation between the physical body and a spiritual entity and suggested the latter interacted with the body's mechanics to control its behavior.

"The agency, or the ability to make choices and

decisions, comes from within us, and not from some mysterious outside ghostly force," she said in a televised interview preserved for posterity on YouTube.

Amid these contemplations, she became an agnostic, believing it superior to both theism and atheism. "Agnostic beliefs allow for more open-ended and critical thinking," she said. Noting that theism is rooted in faith, it's "Not a reliable way to know anything," she wrote. She viewed atheism as being as "dogmatic as theism." She has concluded theism and atheism would invariably lead to intolerance and violence. Touting an agnostic approach, she said, "It does not require us to believe or disbelieve in anything, and it allows us to question and explore all possibilities. There are more productive ways to approach the question of God's existence, which is more likely to lead to a more just and equitable world."

On this particular picturesque morning, the sun painted the morning with its golden hues, and Linda Herzog positioned herself by the roadside. Her meticulously secured possessions were inside the confines of a vintage forest green canvas bookbag slung over one shoulder. Looking at the approaching flow of traffic, she extended her thumb. The destination was set, and Washington D.C. beckoned. All she needed was a charitable passerby. Determined to make her journey with the lightest ecological trace, she committed to embark on her objective by hitchhiking. With careful consideration, she allocated three days. Over morning coffee, she had concluded her week-long visit with a fellow researcher she'd first met while studying at Berkley. Her friend lived nestled under the shadows of the rugged Rocky Mountains in a single-room log cabin on the outskirts of Bozeman, Montana. The morning summer air hung crisp around her while she waited.

Forty minutes elapsed. A four-door car glided to a halt, and the passenger window whirred down. The orange Ford Focus wore its history like a patchwork quilt. A mismatched blue hood, gray filler patches on the rear body panels, and a missing hubcap all exposed the battle scars of life. Ellie, a woman in her late forties, possessed twinkling eyes born from a myriad of experiences. In a dulcet and measured voice, she unfolded into quite the storyteller, sharing her battle scars and painting a portrait of her life.

The course of the conversation revealed Ellie to be more than a mere motorist. She was a queer artist whose vibrant youth was spent meandering across the country searching for inspiration and a place where her true self could find solace. Ultimately, Bozeman captured her heart, drawing her in during her late twenties with its reputation for embracing souls skittering on societal fringes. In recounting her journey, Ellie shared universal experiences, stories of love's tender embrace, and the anguish of parting. Her words revealed the struggle of discovering her identity in a world where diversity was all too often rebuffed. Linda listened intently, her heart a refuge for Ellie's narratives, an auditorium of empathy and advice. However, the winding road could only accommodate their exchange for so long. The benevolent journey extended as far as Billings, where they found themselves at a haven for comfort food nestled beside the Sassy Biscuit Company. A quaint sign crowned the diner, Uncle Bunny's.

The diner was busy with a constant flux of people coming and going. At ten past twelve, the next segment of her journey began. A towering, jacked-up, long-bed pickup with oversized tires and a Cummins turbo diesel engine made its presence known on the road's shoulder. A logo comprised of two horses and illegible cursive writing emblazoned the sides of the bed. The truck exuded the impression of a midlife metamorphosis, a cocky persona accustomed to playing life, perhaps a combination of the two. Its driver, Carlos, occupied the front seat – a middle-aged man whose grin showcased two rows of straight, gleaming white teeth. He wore a tan-colored, beaver fur felt Stetson with a cattleman's style crown. A brown tooled band with a three-piece buckle wound around the base of the break. His concealed eyes behind shades added a layer of mystique.

A combination, if ever there was one, she concluded.

Carlos' world was straightforward, devoid of unnecessary frills. He was a man of few words, a no-nonsense character molded by life on a nearby ranch. His present course pointed him toward Minneapolis. Their journey unfolded, and a detour emerged in their conversation. Carlos bared a raw truth about his infidelity. The admission unveiled a habit that had morphed into a full-time hobby. The stories of his amorous conquests caused her discomfort, and she felt vulnerable and insecure. She found herself inching ever closer to the passenger door.

Carlos eventually guided the truck into a Flying J gas station on the edge of Bismarck, North Dakota. The pit stop offered more than fuel with a realm of practical amenities. Diesel and gasoline flowed, beyond which there were electric charging stations. Hot showers beckoned weary drivers, and a lounge promised brief respites from the road's monotony while a public laundry stood ready to restore the fabric of cleanliness. A Subway sandwich restaurant offered sustenance, and the property housed parking spots for the Interstate's behemoths, the eighteen-wheelers. Linda wasted no time taking her cue to step out of the cab.

"I have to use the ladies' room," she said while holding her bookbag.

With no intention of returning, she fastidiously surveyed her surroundings for a suitable hideaway. She selected an alternative exit door from the one by which she had entered and found a hidden niche behind the colossal wheel of a Peterbilt, complete with a custom sleeper. Nestled in her newly discovered refuge, she peered through the trailer's understory and observed Carlos and his truck. The passage of ten minutes marked an ephemeral interval during which her world held its breath. Then, as if scripted by her urging, the long bed dissolved from view, departing the gas station to rejoin the Interstate from the on-ramp.

By this time, the Peterbilt's driver, Rusty, tapped her on the shoulder.

"Everything alright, young lady."

"Yes. Thank you. I thought it was a good time to leave my friend behind. So, I dipped out of sight."

"If you're needing a ride, I'm headed toward Chicago. If that suits, I'm more than happy to oblige."

Rusty's six-foot-four frame soared, accommodating the breadth of his substantial beer belly with an air of nonchalance. A salt and pepper-colored, walrus-styled mustache adorned the expanse above his upper lip and bestowed an air of seasoned independence. His cheeks and chin bore the signature shadow of someone needing a shave, further testimony to a rugged lifestyle. His attire consisted of faded dungarees, while a once-vibrant red and black plaid flannel shirt hung untucked, evoking memories of days long past. A gunmetal-hued, waxed trucker jacket draped his form, its breast pocket proudly brandishing a patch bearing the double-A emblem of the "All-Americans," the insignia of the U.S. Army's Eighty-Second Airborne. The division was synonymous with dangerous parachute assault maneuvers behind enemy lines. A mesh baseball cap clung to the top of his head, its orange front panel boldly embossed with the word "Stihl" in resolute white capital letters.

"My son was Eighty-Second," she said in a truthful-sounding, reflex lie induced by her minutes-old trauma. "A lift would be more than appreciated, sir."

Still traumatized, she slept for the better part of the next twelve hours. She woke up just before the truck pulled into the Pilot Travel Center in Bensenville, just west of O'Hare.

THE FLAT TIRE

"This here's the end of the line, little lady. There's a Super 8 just on the other side of Mickey Dee's if you need to keep sleeping."

Adjusting herself to sit up straight, she asked, "What time is it?"

"Seven-thirty. The sun's been up for an hour. There's no clouds in the sky, so the temperature should be into the high seventies by lunchtime."

"Can I buy you a breakfast sandwich and coffee? You've been so kind, letting me sleep the whole way."

"Pleasure, ma'am. I'm good. You enjoy the rest of your trip and try to stay safe. Watch your step as you get out. We're high up."

She waved goodbye to Rusty from the ground and walked toward an area where passenger cars exited the facility. The fourth driver of Linda's journey introduced her to the vibrant presence of Alex, an exuberant young woman with radiating energy. Linda found herself drawn to the captivating hue of her eyes. Their encounter carried an unspoken recognition, a shared understanding beyond words. Over the span of the next five hours, the air echoed with an animated exchange fueled by Alex's boundless enthusiasm. Her passion was palpable, encapsulating her role as an activist steadfastly dedicated to the cause of LGBTQ+ rights.

The road transformed into an expansive fresco for discourse. Each mile served as a brushstroke, and each sentence contributed to the composition of impassioned words. The air was filled with a narrative of debates contended and victories cherished. Linda listened to the one-sided symphony of thoughts and ideals, a virtually uninterrupted stream of narration spewing from Alex's mind like magma propelled toward the Earth's surface by pressure and uncontainable heat. Even though Linda's own story remained untold during the flurry of words, she couldn't help but appreciate the potency of Alex's mission and the resonance it held in her heart.

In Sylvania, Ohio, Linda's next ride unveiled itself from the back seat of a sedan occupied by front-seated twins in their mid-thirties. On their way to Philadelphia, they announced in unison, that they planned to stop in Dubois, Pennsylvania, to spend the night and finish the drive the following morning. The rhythmic cadence of rubber on asphalt filled the hushed interior. Silence prevailed save for sporadic inquiry about origins and vocations. Perhaps the twins, having spent a lifetime together entwined in an unbreakable bond, had run out of conversation with themselves and everyone else. The three rolled into the parking of the Dubois Hampton Inn minutes before dusk trundled into the night. After checking into the hotel, the three went to eat at the nearby Pizza Hut. Beyond what toppings to choose for the deep dish, the meal continued in relative silence with an ambiance punctuated by the clattering of cutlery against plates.

The following morning, Linda woke early and waited in the lobby. Morning's light cast its long shadows over the parking lot. She noticed a man standing beside his car, emitting an aura of uncertainty, perplexed by the enigma of a flat tire. Her innate instinct to assist drove her outside. With a reassuring nod, she gently guided him aside and assumed a dominant role.

From the recesses of the trunk, Linda retrieved the spare tire and jack, setting the stage for a mechanical ballet. Her hands danced with deftness as she maneuvered the jack, the car's weight lifting slowly from the ground. With a determined grace, she lowered herself onto her knees, undeterred by the prospect of dirt and scrapes. The wheel lug nuts yielded under her confident touch, and the tire change began to take shape under the auspices of her experience.

The man gaped in awe, a spectator to her prowess. A comment escaped his lips, a reflection of his gratitude tainted with a tinge of surprise as if her capability had challenged his machoism. Her response was an internal sigh, a decision to let such remarks slide, a recognition to let her actions speak volumes beyond the confines of gender roles through performative acts. In their exchange of words, it turned out that he was headed to Washington, D.C., and would be willing to take her along. By the time she was lowering the jack, the twins came out into the parking lot. There were gracious hugs, and the twins departed in their sedan.

By mid-afternoon, the journey's last leg concluded, and Linda was deposited at the doorstep of her D.C. hotel. In the quietude of the room, she lay on top of her bed and allowed herself the luxury of introspection, her thoughts drifting like autumn leaves in the wind.

At 5:15 p.m., she stepped out into the thrumming heartbeat of the city; the late afternoon air held an air of expectancy. The bustling rush-hour streets whispered promises of exploration, each step an invitation to unravel some type of enigma. Linda wandered in pursuit of a place to savor a cup of coffee, a simple pleasure to encapsulate the essence of new beginnings. She had arrived in time; now, all that was left was to wait for tomorrow.

MARTIN

IMAM MARTIN WAS GETTING ON IN YEARS AND, BY ALL accounts, was locked into his golden years. Back when he was born, the landscape looked different. The difference could be noted in terms of societal changes and the rapid growth of urbanized areas that ate away at the country's green pastures. He was born soon after a twister threatened Marshalltown, Iowa, a city in the center of the state that found a way to blend manufacturing and farming communities. The Devil's chainsaw tore through the city's outskirts before veering northwest toward Wandering Creek Golf Course and the satellite town of Marietta. At the hospital, the neonatal nurse mentioned how the drop in barometric pressure hastened the "bundle of joy with the arresting smile into this world."

His father, John, was a Baptist minister and a civil rights activist who had been born in Tupelo, Mississippi. Soon after Martin's birth, John moved the family to Saint Louis,

Missouri. Martin's mother, Mary Grace, hailed from Martinique in the Caribbean, which is how he'd come by his name. Martin had a happy childhood, though his family faced frequent harassment due to John's activism. When Martin was four years old, supremacists burned down the family's home. Unharmed but shaken, the family relocated to another town. Still, harassment never seemed too far away. Tragically, his father was found dead soon after Martin started fifth grade. Although John's death was ruled an accident, the family thought otherwise and had difficulty accepting the official account.

Mary Grace's heart was broken, and she struggled to provide for her children. She suffered a psychotic break when Martin was twelve and was committed to a behavioral health facility. Martin and his siblings were split up and placed in foster care. For the remainder of his formative years, Martin was never able to settle, not because of his behavior or attributes but because child welfare moved him from family to family and from one state to the next.

He was a bright student and, against all odds, avoided the gravitational pull toward the miscreants and societal misfits that would go through school life as a student in name only. His academic studies took the occasional setback when he transitioned from one school to the next. Each new school somehow managed to have a different curriculum, and the frequent change was both a distraction and academically unsettling.

He was with his first foster family for three weeks. The

father broke his leg in three places in an accidental fall on an icy patch of sidewalk. His lack of agility cost him his job. The loss of income brought social services to the door, leading Martin to a new placement family. His time with the second family fared no better. He spent a little over six months with his third family, but they ran into issues when their older son was arrested for dealing tainted fentanyl imported from China. No matter what, fate always seemed to intervene and create a disruption. Finally, after years of bouncing around, feeling unsettled and lost, Martin decided to drop out of school and drop out of being fostered. Despite graduating near the top of his class after his sophomore high school year, the straw had broken the camel's back. Without someone vested in his life plan to watch over him, guide him, and act as a mentor, and without a caring school counselor and being fatherless, he decided enough was enough. He would no longer put himself at the mercy of being shipped around from one family to another, so he bid the foster and educational systems adieu.

    He tried living on the streets of Boston and New York City, working odd jobs here and there to get by. By the age of seventeen, Martin was arrested. Other than being in the wrong place at the wrong time, he hadn't done anything amiss. After a quick court hearing, he was sentenced to juvenile detention, nothing more than a foster home built for scale. Resentment born of the injustices he'd encountered shaped his outlook until he found purpose and meaning through Islam.

Once he was back on the streets, he landed a job as a busboy at a second-rate but busy restaurant. One of the cooks took a shine to Martin and started educating him about the Nation of Islam. He was enticed by what he heard and spent his free time reading about the organization. However, Martin decided not to join the Nation formally. While the emphasis on Black pride and self-sufficiency struck a chord, and messages of empowerment appealed to him, he ultimately felt uneasy with how some of the stories juxtaposed his beliefs.

Martin's last name had been Johnson, a name that carried the weight of his family's painful history as enslaved people and constantly reminded him of the atrocities inflicted upon his ancestors. With his newfound knowledge of the Nation of Islam, Martin decided to shed the burden of being tied to an unknown slave master who had claimed ownership over his family. In doing so, he experienced a profound sense of liberation. He reclaimed his identity and positioned himself to forge a path of his own. In its place, he chose nothing. He chose not to have a last name at all. Without a last name, he had gained a sense of agency. He embraced the opportunity to shape his own narrative and create a future untethered from anyone's past.

With no last name, Martin went back to school and was accepted into Boston University's Islamic Studies program. He would graduate with *Summa Cum Laude* honors for both his undergraduate and postgraduate degrees, a testament to his unwavering dedication and academic excellence throughout his educational journey.

During his time at BU, he was warmly welcomed by the faculty members and other students. He finally found a place where people had his back. The classes gave him access to all aspects of Islam. From its early history to its modern manifestations, he delved into the Qur'an, Hadith, Islamic philosophy, Sufism, Islamic art, and contributions made by Islamic scholars to academic fields of knowledge.

Martin found himself captivated by the insightful lectures and discussions. The professors were not merely teachers; they were also mentors. He received guidance and was encouraged to explore his own beliefs. Beyond the classroom, the program organized regular events, seminars, and guest lectures that brought prominent scholars, religious leaders, and experts to campus. Attending the gatherings with enthusiasm, he found himself engaged in vibrant debates and forging connections.

One of the highlights was a study-abroad opportunity that allowed him to immerse himself in the culture and traditions of a Muslim-majority country. He seized on the opportunity to experience firsthand the living heritage of Islam. His time abroad deepened his understanding of the faith and enriched his appreciation for its diversity. Throughout his academic journey, the experience transformed his horizons and nurtured his empathy and compassion. He learned about the history and theology of Islam as well as the lives and experiences of Muslims around the world; it represented his dedication to fostering mutual respect and understanding among people from diverse backgrounds.

However, his path to enlightenment was not without its challenges. Initially, the depth of classical Arabic required in interpreting religious texts proved daunting. The intricacies of grammar and the nuances of language required perseverance and dedication to master. Navigating sensitive topics also tested his resolve. The department encouraged open discussions, delving into controversial issues that led to spirited debates. Martin witnessed the clash of different perspectives, a reminder that the quest for understanding required humility and open-mindedness.

When he walked across the graduation stage to receive his master's degree with pride, he carried both a degree and an appreciation for the beauty of Islam and the intricacies of humanity. The program had molded him into an ambassador, equipping him to build bridges of understanding in a world yearning for unity.

Martin matured into an emissary of peace and a source of knowledge for those seeking answers. His journey of exploration taught him that while different paths may appeal to individuals based on their circumstances and experiences, it was crucial to embrace the essence of love, tolerance, and understanding. Islam had given him an unshackled sense of belonging to a global community transcending race, nationality, and ethnicity. Islam also allowed him to continue cherishing the values of love, compassion, and self-improvement he'd learned from his parents as a young boy.

By the time Martin turned twenty-seven, he was a changed man; savvy, he was both street-smart and book-smart. He knew he was leading a life of purpose. He relocated to Harlem in New York City and attended the Harlem Islamic Center on Adam Clayton Powell, Jr. Boulevard. The confidence and dignity of the attending Muslims struck him. They didn't smoke, drink, or do drugs. They spoke about people of color, not as victims but as leaders.

Martin's unwavering dedication and relentless pursuit of knowledge further propelled him. His profound commitment to learning and spiritual growth eventually led him to embrace a noble calling as an imam by his thirty-fifth birthday. He had shown his ability to demonstrate knowledge, piety, and the ability to lead and serve the community effectively in matters of faith and spirituality. With a compassionate heart and a mind enriched with wisdom, Martin's impact reverberated far beyond the confines of his local community. His reputation as a spiritual guide and teacher of profound insight spread throughout the country, drawing seekers from near and far.

In his role as an imam, Martin became a beacon of hope. He offered solace and support to those in need. His empathetic nature and innate ability to connect with others created a safe space for people to share their joys and struggles, confident that they would find understanding and encouragement. He went far beyond simply leading prayers; he became a source of inspiration and guidance for his congregation. His sermons resonated with a profound sense of sincerity, weaving together timeless Islamic teachings with practical wisdom for navigating the complexities of modern life.

Seekers and believers flocked to his mosque. They found a haven of spiritual enlightenment where the light of faith illuminated their paths. Martin's profound understanding of the Qur'an and Hadith and his gentle demeanor left a lasting impression on all who crossed his path.

His tireless dedication to personal growth and continuous learning became a testament to the transformative power of faith. His journey from a convert to an imam exemplified the beauty of Islam's teachings, which nurtured a sense of purpose, belonging, and compassion.

The Harlem community found an imam and a spiritual leader who exemplified Islam's essence: a path of love, understanding, and service to humanity. Through his guidance, they rediscovered the profound depths of their faith, reminding them that Islam was not merely a belief system but a way of life fostering unity and goodness for all.

In his autobiography, *Winning at Any Cost Is Not the Goal*, he described his journey of personal courage, passion, and perseverance to face adversity. Martin became one of the most influential leaders in human rights. His story and inspiring words resonated and motivated each new generation that sought to fight for freedom and equality. His follow-up book was also a *New York Times* bestseller, *Human: What a Great Story!*

In both of his books, he recounted his youth, how he often tried to hide his struggles and put up walls to avoid

THE FLAT TIRE

being judged, whether by the color of his skin, his inability not to strike out in a baseball game, or his knowledge of a given subject. He stated, "I know honesty and vulnerability are so important."

He promoted spending time developing interests and passions to make others more interesting and to bring balance into their lives. He offered suggestions such as exercising, reading, volunteering, and learning to play a musical instrument. He recommended working on self-confidence and self-esteem, finding something to make people feel good about themselves each and every day. He offered advice on setting small goals and acknowledging personal victories, encouraging people to step out of their comfort zones. "Loving yourself helps you develop healthier relationships," he wrote.

He believed in open and honest communication, and that people should feel comfortable to share needs, wants, feelings, and opinions. He advocated a philosophy of "Listening without judgment." He insisted that "the ability to communicate in a constructive way is the foundation for leading a meaningful life."

"Be willing to say no," he'd say. He preached that, when necessary, people should set boundaries and not feel guilty when doing so while respecting the boundaries of others. Healthy boundaries, in his mind, led to healthy relationships. Boundaries naturally paved the way to finding shared interests and creating quality time with others. When engaging with others, he encouraged his students to make the time to connect by giving their full and utmost attention. Sharing details of your lives, hopes, dreams, struggles, and victories served to shape what he would call, "fruitful bonds that tear down malice and self-interest."

He viewed life as a team sport where you shouldn't hesitate to get help from others. "For living life alone is to live life without a mark," he told his congregations. He also advised how, "seeking counseling or advice from others is a strength, especially when you are down and struggling." He continued, "Be willing to compromise when you disagree. Look for solutions where you both can feel heard and respected. Be open to perspectives other than your own. No two people will agree on everything, so compromise is key."

In his book, *As Luck Would Have It*, he provided a path for living that didn't rely on luck. From his observation, he thought that too many relied on luck for too many things – whether the luck was blind, accidental, sentient, or private. He explained blind luck as involving things entirely outside your control. "Where you are born, who you are born to, certain health conditions, and so forth. All of these are outside of your control." He would explain accidental luck as "begotten happenstance. When going about your business, hustling and bustling, doing this and doing that, the more you do, the more you're likely to stumble into something." He simply described sentient luck as putting yourself in the right place at the right time. "You can position yourself for lucky breaks by learning to spot them from a mile away because of your knowledge and experience." And finally, private luck stemmed from your

THE FLAT TIRE

own unique attributes that attracted specific luck to you. He'd say, "This type of luck favors eccentrics and those with outlandish lifestyles."

In a *New York Times* article, he told the journalist, "It's hard to get lucky sitting on your behind, watching television at home. It's far easier to get lucky when you're out there getting engaged and learning: reaching out to speak with new people one-on-one, getting into a dialog on social media, and actively participating in your community. These are all meaningful ways to generate luck without hoping it creeps under your door and into your living room to find you." On a personal note, he added that he, "struggled with health, but luck wasn't going to come his way if he just stayed at home and waited."

In more recent years, Martin had been using a tour bus to drive around the country, delivering speeches and leading prayer sessions. The previous evening, he was in Saint Louis to deliver a speech on diversity and equity at an interfaith community center. In the morning, at 6:00 a.m., Martin and his seven entourage members boarded the tour bus and hit the road heading for Washington, D.C. The journey was scheduled to take sixteen hours, with several rest stops and prayer breaks planned. The ride would take them on I-70 through Indianapolis, Columbus, Ohio, and just south of Pittsburgh before they would cut over to I-270 and then I-495.

Martin gazed out the tinted window at the passing farms and fields of middle America, lost in thought. A sudden deceleration roused him from his reverie. The bus pulled over to the side of the road and stopped.

"What's going on?" Martin asked of the driver.

"Looks like there's an elderly couple with a flat tire, sir."

The driver added, "They've got their hazards on."

"Well, we'll have to help them then, won't we?" Martin said.

Martin stood up out of his seat and addressed his staff.

"Gentlemen, it looks like we've got some folks in need of our assistance. Let's grab the jack and their spare, and give them a hand."

"We've got this, sir. We don't need you over-exerting yourself and jeopardizing your place on the list."

Martin followed his staff off the bus and over to the elderly couple's sedan.

"Afternoon, folks. Looks like you could use a little help?" Martin said with a smile.

The couple's faces lit up with relief and gratitude. With the extra hands, swapping out the flat tire for the spare only took a few minutes. Rather than merely standing by, Martin seized the opportunity to engage in conversation with the couple.

"Bless you all," the woman said after everything had been fixed.

Martin tipped his cap and waved as they pulled away, continuing their journey. A few hours later, the bus slowed again. But this time, a woman flagged them down with panic showing all across her face.

THE FLAT TIRE

"Please, help me! Our car has broken down, and my friend's in labor. The baby's coming!"

Once more, the entourage sprang into action.

The men helped both women up the steps of the bus. The pregnant woman was breathing heavily, her face contorted in pain, and the men cleared space for her.

"Come on, let's get them both onto the bus. Easy now. Let them sit here," Martin said. He turned to the driver. "Looks like we'll need to get this woman to the nearest hospital! Is the GPS working? Just keep breathing, ma'am. We'll have you at the hospital soon."

Within fifteen minutes, they arrived at a small rural community hospital. Martin's staff helped get the woman, now moaning louder, into the hospital emergency room. The staff whisked her away, and Martin gave the details of her situation to the attending nurses. Leaving both women in capable hands, he left the hospital to resume his journey, but first, he called a towing and car repair service to collect the vehicle. Quietly, he gave the service his credit card number and told them to deliver the repaired vehicle to the hospital.

The bus arrived in D.C. behind schedule, but no one had any regrets.

"There's nothing more important than that. Each life we impact, no matter how small, matters," Martin said as he handed out the room keys to his men. "I hope Allah will bless you with sweet dreams tonight. May Allah grant all your prayers and requests. Gentlemen, I bid you all a very good night. Good night!"

PART II

HERMANOS

IN WASHINGTON, D.C., THE PRESTIGIOUS LAW OFFICES OF Moytoy, Bissouma, Porro, Son, and Postecoglou can be found steps away from the White House in the esteemed Hamilton Square area. When it comes to constitutional law, their name booms as a masterpiece of expectation and dominance. Occupying thirty thousand square feet of meticulously fabricated faux Koa wood-paneled office space, they aren't just another white shoe D.C. law firm; they are ecologically minded. Moreover, the firm represents a global empire of legal prowess.

Whispered conversations among elite circles paint them as the first and foremost option for those with substantially deep pockets. Their legacy is not merely defined by the legal battles they've fought but by the realm of victories they craft.

The early risers were already milling around at The Hotel Washington just across the street. Those fortunate enough to have knees unburdened by years of strain were returning from a refreshing morning jog around The Mall. Moving through the lobby towards the row of elevators, each person was met with multiple cheerful greetings, such as "May you have a pleasant morning and a wonderful day ahead." The ambient noise had grown, signifying the hotel's shift into a lively, dynamic hub of activity with a vigorous pace worthy of a bustling metropolis.

Upstairs, Otto LaMacchia was still in his bedroom finishing up the morning's *New York Times* crossword puzzle. He sat in a comfortable brown leather chair with minimal scuff marks and began to think about his appetite. His corner room, a deluxe king, was opulent and furnished in a modern style with quaint touches to provide a homey feel. The impressive one-of-a-kind headboard featured inlaid cherry blossoms made of exotic woods, mother of pearl, and abalone – a reminder to the occupant of the capital's reawakening during springtime festivals. Laying down the iPad face up on the side table, he pushed himself off the soft cushion and walked a few steps over to the window that rose a handful of stories above the sidewalks on Fifteenth and F. While he had to make do with a west-facing view, he was afforded a grandstand view of the South Lawn.

Remarkable, he thought.

His heart was heavy with the weight of the day's significance as a tide of reflective thoughts washed over him. He recalled the shock and disbelief reverberating nationwide and worldwide that day. Despite the overwhelming pain of loss felt by most, a certain unity arose from the ashes in the aftermath. At the time, he viewed the carnage as a personal call to arms to imbue faith in his parish faithful.

From the bedroom window, he saw more than just a physical space; he saw a testament to the courage and determination that had rebuilt a shattered nation. In the distance, an un-fluttering flag rested at half-staff. He spoke a prayer.

"In the name of the Father, and of the Son, and of the Holy Spirit, as I stand here on this solemn day, I am reminded of the fragility of life and the resilience of the human spirit. I offer this prayer from the depths of my heart, seeking solace, guidance, and unity in these reflective moments. Grant me the strength to carry the memories of those who were lost with grace and reverence. May their stories remind me to cherish every moment and embrace the bonds of love that connect us all. Bless the families and friends who continue to feel the ache of their absence. Surround them with your comfort and give them the courage to find healing and hope. Amidst the pain, I recall the countless acts of heroism and selflessness that emerged from out of the darkness. Help me to carry those stories as beacons of light, inspiring me to be a source of kindness and compassion in the world. Guide our leaders with wisdom, empathy, and the vision to build a future that honors the memory of those who were lost. May they work tirelessly to promote peace, unity, and understanding among all people. In this quiet moment, I also pray for unity among nations and faiths. May we find common ground, recognizing that our shared humanity is stronger than our differences. We are all created equal in your image. Lord, grant me the strength to be an instrument of peace and a source of hope in a world terribly divided. Fill my heart with faith; may goodness prevail. Through our collective efforts, guide us to remake a world where love triumphs over hate and where unity triumphs over division. In the shadow of the South Lawn, under the open sky, I offer this prayer for all those who were affected by the events on this day and for the world at large. May your light guide us forward, and may we always strive to honor the memory of those we have lost. We ask this through our Lord Jesus Christ. Amen."

Satisfied with his inspection and introspection of the outside world, he turned and walked toward the wardrobe, where his suit jacket hung neatly on one of the hotel's fine padded hangers. Removing the jacket, he momentarily placed the jacket on top of the quilted bed cover. He maneuvered to the nightstand and picked up his jeweled crucifix ring, sliding it onto his left ring finger. Admiring the ring, he offered another short prayer of thanksgiving then picked up his jacket and put it on.

From the table beside the brown leather chair, he picked up his smartphone, putting it in the lower inside pocket of the suit jacket, and placed his iPad inside the room's built-in safe. At the door, he scanned the bedroom one final time, ensuring he'd collected everything he wished to take with him. The adjacent wall next to the door featured a large full-length mirror.

The ornate gilded mirror stood as an exquisite piece of artistry and function. Its frame, meticulously crafted and adorned with lavish detailing, reflected light from the windows. The dimensions offered a full view of one's reflection from head to toe. The glass, devoid of imperfections, was flawlessly polished and afforded a crystal-clear reflection. Anyone looking at it was reminded, in no uncertain terms and in a Descartes-like manner, that they existed: "*Ergo es*, therefore you are."

He stared deeper into the mirror and was pleased with what he saw reflected – a man of honor, faith, and trust, a man who had worked hard, and a man who had attained his position because it was earned. Satisfied, he left his room, bound for breakfast and the exclusive restaurant, Hermanos, located on the hotel's top floor.

"Good morning, sir," said the *maître d'*.

"And, a very good morning to…" Otto took a quick look at the gentleman's name tag worn on his jacket's breast pocket, "You too, Jabari. I hope your day is off to a wonderful start?"

"Yes, thank you, sir. May I have your room number?"

"D14."

"Ah," the *maître d'* said. He scanned the approved patron list in front of him. "Forgive me, Cardinal. Right this way, please. We have a table waiting for you over by the window. I trust your trip to the capital was uneventful?"

"Perfectly fine. A straightforward trip. No trouble at all." Otto said more with a smirk than a smile.

"I've been listening to the news about Geronimo. Awful. All of those communities."

"I've been keeping everyone in my prayers. It's important that we all have faith during these troubling times," Otto said.

Pulling out the seat for the cardinal, Jabari said, "Here we are. Your server will be with you momentarily. Enjoy your breakfast."

The restaurant windows faced east. Otto could feel the early morning rays against his face. He felt relaxed and closed his eyes to focus on the remnants of this year's summer warmth.

"Good morning, Cardinal. How are we today?"

The server's voice startled Otto, causing him to jump in his seat. His eyes sprang open, and he moved his head to look in her direction. The waitress looked young, very young. She was thin, her face gaunt, but her mesmerizing green eyes and dark black eyebrows appeared to shout, "Take a good hard look at me. I could be the one!"

Her auburn hair was worn in a ponytail. Short bangs covered her forehead. Her pants were black and made from three-season wool. The hotel didn't permit black jeans or khakis. A clean, black, three-pocket full bistro apron encircled her thin waist and fell just above her ankles. Her shoes were flat Mary Jane's over plain black cotton socks. A five-pleat formal dress shirt with a wing collar and French cuffs covered her torso. Her cufflinks were knotted and made from a stretchy elastane-viscose yarn.

"My apologies, Cardinal. May I offer you the menu? Would you like some coffee while I give you time to look it over?"

"Thank you, my child. A latte would be nice. Otherwise, a coffee with half-and-half will suit just fine."

Otto began to look around the dining room. He was the only seated patron. Elegance reigned supreme across the parade of two dozen or so linen-clothed tables. The grandeur offered an atmosphere of refined splendor. The intricate architectural details – from the leafy crown molding gracing the ceiling to the ornate columns – were exacting; everything exuded an air of regal sophistication. The soft glow of crystal chandeliers, suspended from the ceiling like a hanging waterfall of light, cast an inviting ambiance. The multitude of facets captured and bent the light and it appeared to perform an intricate dance of radiance across the gleaming marble floors.

Each table was adorned with exquisite silverware, crystal stemware, and delicate porcelain plates poised to accept omelets, sausages, and toast. The tufted dining chairs were upholstered in a regal purple velvet, with an intricate flower pattern of the same color that invited guests to settle in and ready themselves for satisfying conversation and an indulgent feast. Richly-hued jacquard drapery adorned with golden tassels framed the bank of large windows covered with linen sheers, softening the morning rays to add a savory mystique to the setting. It would be another hour before the hushed whispers and the gentle clinking of utensils would create a harmonious background soundtrack as guests, dressed in their finest daywear, engaged in a variety of animated conversations. Attentive servers, clad in immaculate uniforms, would glide gracefully between patrons, tending to every need with discreet professionalism epitomizing the pinnacle of hospitality.

The dining room's centerpiece was a grand, meticulously crafted sideboard with a display of tall vases holding exotic flowers of vibrant color. In this space, every detail, from the lavish *décor* to the impeccable service, was carefully planned to create an experience meant to transform breakfast into the most important meal of the day. This place was a sanctuary for culinary artistry to meet architectural elegance where guests could be treated to a utopian, sensory awakening.

The menu, presented on thick embossed parchment paper, was free from any food stains or marks and was another example of the hotel's commitment to excellence. Each dish was described with meticulous detail to evoke visions of flavor and texture. The "Gourmet Continental" offered a sumptuous array of freshly baked pastries and artisanal breads in a variety of sliced thicknesses to suit any personal preference. Whispering promises of caloric excess, the crispy croissants, delicate *pain au chocolat*, and flaky Danish would be presented side by side with a selection of house-made preserves, rich European-styled salted and unsalted butters, and exquisite fruit compotes.

The "Epicurean Breakfast" offered an alternative

temptation for those seeking a heartier option. A kosher "Truffle-infused Eggs Benedict à l'Orange," where velvety poached eggs nestled atop finely sliced Madeira oranges resting on a delicate, buttered English muffin adorned with glistening strands of truffle and a luscious drizzled hollandaise sauce sounded tantalizing. Other dishes such as the "Lobster and Avocado Omelet," the "Luxury Pancake," and the "Vitality Morning Harvest" were all listed under the heading "Suggestions," providing each guest an open invitation for anything their hungry heart might desire.

The server's soft voice interrupted his perusal. "I have your latte, Cardinal. Are you ready, or would you like a few more minutes? I asked our barista to include an extra shot of espresso. I hope that's okay. You seemed like you could use an extra boost this morning."

"God bless you. No, no. I'm ready to give you my order now. May I have two soft-boiled eggs and a slice of unseeded rye toast with the crusts removed and sliced into half-inch strips, if it's not too much to ask? Oh, and a pot of marmalade."

"Certainly, Cardinal. I'll let the chef know and get that started for you right away."

Otto's smartphone gently vibrated in his inside jacket pocket. Pulling the phone out, he read the text message. Meanwhile, the next guest wanting breakfast had walked up to the host stand.

"Good morning," Jabari said.

"Good morning," came back the reply. "A table for one, please."

"May I have your room number?"

"D13."

"How strange. Our other guest is right next to your room. Ah, yes. Rabbi Rahabi. It's a pleasure to have you join us this morning. If you'll follow me, please."

Jabari led Ezekiel to the same table where Cardinal LaMacchia was sitting, waiting for his eggs and toast. Jabari pulled out one of the other chairs from the table and instructed him to take a seat by simply issuing the word, "Please."

Otto looked up from his phone, confused.

"It was a table for one," Ezekiel said to Jabari.

"Yes, yes, but we were given instructions to seat all of Ms. Moytoy's guests together if they came in for breakfast this morning. Both you and Cardinal LaMacchia are guests of Ms. Moytoy," Jabari said.

"Thank you for clarifying," Ezekiel said, Jabari took his leave. The rabbi looked at Otto and extended his hand. "I hadn't realized there were others," he said. "I'm Rabbi Ezekiel Rahabi, and you're Cardinal? I didn't catch the last name."

"LaMacchia. But, please just call me Otto," the Cardinal said, succumbing to the feeling that control was evading him. *And I haven't even had a chance to dip a slice of toast into my runny egg. Now, I've got to watch my table manners,* he thought. "A rabbi! I assumed Ms. Moytoy's meeting might involve others, but having company for breakfast is a welcome distraction."

"Yes, thank you. Please, call me Eli." They both stood and

THE FLAT TIRE

shook hands, saying, "It's nice to meet you," at the same time. They sat down.

The waitress returned to the table with another menu in her hand. She looked at Otto and said, "I apologize for the wait, it'll just be a few more minutes." She then looked at Ezekiel. "May I get you started with some tea or coffee?" She handed him the menu. "I'll give you a few minutes to look things over."

Ezekiel saw that she looked young, very young. Her mesmerizing green eyes and dark black eyebrows appeared to whisper at him, "Go on, take a deep good look at me. If there's nothing on the menu for you, you can eat me!"

"Thank you, miss. Green tea if you have," he said.

As the waitress left, Eli said to Otto, "Strange eyes."

"I hadn't noticed," said Otto.

"Actually, she reminds me a little of one of my *bat mitzvah* students. The other week, we were discussing the story of Jonah, and I asked this particular student, 'What's the difference between ignorance and apathy?' She had the audacity to answer, 'I don't know, and I don't care.'"

They both laughed.

"So, where'd you come in from?" Otto asked.

"Jersey."

"Were you able to arrive at a reasonable time?"

UNREASONABLE TIMES

The prior evening, the *Ma'ariv* service at Kesher Israel was scheduled to start at 7:00 p.m. The three-story brick building was over one hundred years old and located in the northwest quadrant of the city on N Street. Eli calculated the drive shouldn't take more than fifteen minutes, perhaps twenty if the traffic was heavier than expected. A quick scan of his smartphone revealed Uncle Bunny's Kosher Diner was located around the corner from the *shul* on 28th Street. Suddenly, the thought of indulging in a hearty portion of comfort food became enticing; its promise of contentment resonated with an undeniable allure.

Eli had settled into his hotel bedroom. It wasn't home, but the bed seemed comfortable enough. The soft murmur of CNN permeated the room. Though the television's volume was barely audible, it cast an amiable backdrop to his setting. His attire had been hung neatly and tucked

THE FLAT TIRE

away, while his toiletries adorned the bathroom sink with meticulous order. Though the hour was not yet pressing, a sense of punctuality nudged him forward. *Better to be thirty minutes early than a single minute late,* he reasoned and readied himself for departure.

He gathered his car keys from the table next to the oversized brown leather chair and patted his pockets to ensure he was in possession of his wallet and phone. The wallet was placed in his rear pant pocket, and the phone was located in his right inside jacket pocket. He was scrupulous about never using the left. He maintained an ongoing fear about what the phone's emitted radiation might do to his heart if nestled within close proximity. Officially, the level of RF radiation was regulated and kept within safety limits, but he was of the opinion that he was never personally consulted as to what constituted safe. While he was never an electrical engineer, he knew how to dig into a product's downside risks from his time on Wall Street. He was sufficiently astute to understand what "the effects of long-term exposure remain inconclusive" meant. Furthermore, since his redemption and reformation, he held a better appreciation for his finite time on this planet; he was in no particular rush toward the inevitable.

On his way out of the hotel, he was greeted by various staffers who smiled politely. Some coupled a nod along with their grin. The gentlemen at the concierge desk offered additional pleasantries, "Have a good evening, sir," along with a beaming row of straight white teeth.

The entrance to the hotel's subterranean parking garage could only be reached from the street. Entering the facility, he took the elevator down to the floor where he'd left his Civic. Exiting the elevator, the air was noticeably stagnant, heavy, and humid. The lingering smell of exhaust fumes was undeniable. The rows of parked vehicles represented a medley of preference; many owners weren't afraid to showcase their ostentatious tastes. Notably, his car stood out in the crowd. Like many other patrons, he had backed into the space to simplify pulling out. Apart from his car's vintage, it stood out for two additional reasons. As far as he could tell, it was the only car with a folded piece of paper tucked under a windshield wiper and the only one with a bowie knife sticking out from a front tire – the passenger side.

"Seriously!"

Deciding to take a closer inspection, Eli squatted down to look at the wheel. Forensic expertise wasn't required to ascertain the tire had been slashed. The primary gouge was at least eight inches long. The knife appeared to have been symbolically inserted and left behind as an exclamation point. The tire was flat and far beyond repair, even from a layperson's perspective.

"*Mochkrushys.*"

His attention turned to the paper under his wiper blade. The outside of the fold contained the word "kite" written with a blue ballpoint pen. The writing could only be seen when holding the paper closer to the eye. *Obviously indoctrinated but not overly educated! You'd think they would teach them how to spell the slur correctly,* he thought. He opened the fold and observed the letter was computer-printed using a large double-spaced, courier-styled font. The message, which was scantily read, contained a diatribe of hate and extreme anti-Semitism. He refolded the paper and tore it in half, then again. He kept repeating this process until he could tear no longer.

Mildly disturbed by the overall situation, he looked around to see if anyone was near, which would further signal his physical well-being might be in danger. He saw nothing. He heard nothing outside the drone of the garage's air conditioners. With shaking hands and knees, he returned to the elevator, entered, and pressed the button for the street level. Upon exiting, he took a moment to survey his surroundings before starting the short walk back to the main entrance door. This wasn't the first time he'd been on the receiving end of such atrocities, and he decided, like before, he wasn't going to let it get to him.

Eli returned to the lobby from which he had departed minutes before, and Plan B entered his mind. He walked to the concierge desk, which was still attended by the same gentleman who had wished him a "good evening." His name tag revealed this was Wyclef Jean.

Wyclef Jean was born in Haiti and grew up in poverty and overcrowding on the outskirts of Port-au-Prince. Continuous gang violence caused him to seek refuge in the United States. After spending time in various Floridian cities, he found gainful employment in D.C. Working hard, he eventually acquired a small two-bedroom house in the suburbs and started a family. Now in his late sixties, his hair was short and gray. He stood straight and tall, and his overall appearance evoked a sense of self-pride. He enjoyed life, and he enjoyed his work at the hotel.

Adjusting his *kippah*, Eli reapplied the hairpin attaching his head covering to his hair, and began a conversation with Wyclef Jean. "By any chance, do you have a trashcan handy?" At first, Eli's words were unclear because he was still recovering from his experience and found he had to clear his throat. He revealed the pieces of paper he was still clutching in his hand to the concierge attendant.

"May I? I'll take care of that for you, sir."

"Thank you, Wyclef Jean. Listen, I've run into something unexpected," and proceeded to pull out his wallet and remove his vehicle insurance card. "My car is parked in the hotel garage, but some creature seems to have taken a distinct dislike to my Honda. I now have a flat tire! Perhaps my car exhibited too much rust for their tastes! Who knows? Anyway, I have a roadside assistance service through my car insurance; here's my insurance card with the number to call. Could I possibly trouble you to arrange for my car to be fixed while I go out this evening? Here are my car keys."

"How most unfortunate, sir. Did you perhaps drive over a nail from the street when you entered the garage?"

"No. It definitively wasn't from a nail. One of my tires was slashed. The person was also kind enough to leave behind the knife. Still in the tire. I presume it's a calling card of sorts. The torn paper you just threw out for me was a note left for me on my windshield. It spelled out this wasn't an accident. I'll need a new tire, too."

"Frè a frè," Wyclef Jean said in Haitian Creole. "Brother to brother, too many people in this world are on the receiving end of hate. There's never a good reason for this. I will take care of this for you. Leave everything with me. You go ahead and enjoy your evening as best you can."

Eli thanked Wyclef Jean and walked to the center of the lobby, where he used an app on his phone to request a taxi. He didn't have to wait too long for the car to arrive, and by 6:00 p.m., he closed the passenger door and stood on the sidewalk outside Uncle Bunny's.

Inside, the diner's clientele was diverse, and the atmosphere calm. It wasn't quiet by any means, but it wasn't so loud you'd have trouble hearing yourself think.

"A table for one?" the hostess asked. She looked to be in her mid-thirties and had a distinct haggard appearance. He wasn't to know, but she was working a double shift and would still be greeting guests for another four hours. Bunny's was open twenty-four hours a day but closed its doors during the Jewish Shabbat and high holidays.

Eli nodded.

"Right this way. Is a booth okay, or would you prefer a table? Use the QR code on the table to bring up the menu; your waitperson should be right with you."

"Thank you."

Before he had a chance to bring up the menu, the waitperson came over, placed a glass of water on the table, and asked, "What can I get you?"

"I haven't had..." He caught himself midsentence. He already knew what he wanted anyway. "May I please have a plate with baked beans, two eggs – sunny side up, and French fries? Oh, and some green tea if you have? Thank you." He attempted a smile.

"Coming right up."

That's the thing about diners: simplicity reigned supreme. They were generally no-nonsense, quick, efficient, and absent of frivolous small talk plaguing finer dining establishments. The food came quickly and was placed before him, and words of gratitude spilled from his lips. The waitperson graciously offered further assistance and departed to attend to another customer. He sat motionless and stared at his food. He found himself frozen in time, unable to move while his mind returned to the incident from less than an hour ago. He thought about the lessons the experience could teach. More than anything, he wished he could teach the perpetrators about their wrongs. Catching himself, he redirected his mind's meandering course back to the present. There was no point dwelling any further on the situation, at least for now. He unfurled the paper napkin wrapping the cutlery, and prepared himself to dig in.

The miracle of comfort food was always its satiating experience. It had a knack of balancing the mind and soul and places the world's ills on the back burner.

"Can I get you anything else?"

"No. That was perfect. Thank you. Just the check, please."

THE FLAT TIRE

When Eli entered the synagogue, the time was 6:40 p.m. He knew the time because he had pulled his phone out to silence it. He returned the phone to his jacket pocket and, once more, checked to ensure his *kippah* was in place.

Upon entering the main doorway, his right hand was instinctively drawn towards the *mezuzah* affixed to the doorframe. Grazing the casing with his fingers, he offered a short, silent prayer. The *mezuzah* symbolized faith and identity. It served as a poignant reminder for those crossing the threshold of their connection with tradition and their commitment to living with the faith's precepts. Having entered the building, he felt a palpable sense of sanctity lingering in the air, another reminder of the divine presence permeating time and space. Furthermore, he was immediately greeted.

"You look familiar."

"Rabbi Ezekiel Rahabi." Eli extended his hand.

The man took a moment to ponder the name. "Ah, yes. I've seen some of your ByteSize videos. I thought I recognized you. Very entertaining! Welcome to Kesher Israel."

Their outstretched hands connected, forming a temporary bond between strangers. "I have the privilege of serving as cantor," he said while introducing himself with a smile. His voice resonated with a deep sense of pride and devotion to his role and the support he provided for the local community. "The Rabbi will be delighted to hear you're joining us this evening. We're usually quite well attended during our weekday services. Is this your first time with us?"

After the pleasantries were complete, the cantor pointed to the door Eli should use to enter the sanctuary. In the moderately sized worship room, he noticed the deep-wine-colored seats. Instead of traditional long pews, the sanctuary employed rows of auditorium-styled chairs with flip-up seats, signs of modernization and comfort in an environment reserved for tradition. Not wishing to occupy the seat of a regular, he chose to sit towards the rear and just off to one side. The chair he selected still afforded him a clear view of the *bimah*, the raised platform from which the evening service would be conducted. Over the next fifteen minutes, close to thirty people entered and took their seats. There was only a handful of people sitting together.

The service began, "Blessed are you, Lord our God, Ruler of the Universe, whose word brings on the evening..." It wasn't yet 7:30 p.m. when the service began drawing to a close. Out of the blue, the rabbi announced, "Our cantor has informed me we have a special congregant *davening*, praying with us this evening. He's a social media influencer of the highest order, Rabbi Rahabi from New Jersey." Then, looking at Eli, he said, "Rabbi, I don't wish to impose on you, but could I entice you to come up onto the *bimah* and offer a ByteSize edible for our congregation? It would be a *mitzvah*, a privilege for all of us to hear from you."

Sure, play the mitzvah card and lay a guilt trip on me! Eli thought. "I'd love to, Rabbi. It'll be a privilege."

Eli stood up and rebuttoned his jacket. He pulled down

THE FLAT TIRE

on the hem using both hands to ensure the jacket was hanging correctly before he started to walk. Moving past the three empty seats next to him, he made his way into the aisle. He walked the short twenty or so feet toward the *bimah* and climbed the four steps to the platform's top. As a rabbi, Eli was generally prepared for the unexpected. He could respond to a challenging situation without much effort. But normally, this meant the topic of discussion was handed to him, requiring some words of guidance, congratulations, or consolation. Here, he had to think of a topic on the fly. As he walked towards the other rabbi, a few subjects entered his mind: prison, comfort food, and, of course, flat tires. The rabbis shook hands.

"Thank you, Rabbi. Please..." the other rabbi said, signaling with his hand that his audience awaited.

"*Shalom*, good evening." Looking at the congregation, he said, "What a beautiful *shul* you have here." Then, returning his look to the other rabbi, he said, "Rabbi, thank you for inviting me to speak for a few minutes." It was time to riff, and so he began.

"A funny thing happened on the way to the forum! I probably should have tried to say that while imitating Groucho Marx." He then attempted to mimic Groucho's characteristic hand gestures helping him punctuate one of his gag lines. "However, that particular line comes from the title of Buster Keaton's last movie. Don't get me wrong, I know it was a long time ago, but I can see some of you should have a vague recollection as to who he was!"

Eli took another breath and pulled down on his jacket

again. He rechecked his *kippah*. He felt a little uncomfortable but continued. "I came down to D.C. for a meeting I have tomorrow in Hamilton Square. I had planned to attend this evening's service as we don't have the luxury of holding evening services at my *shul* in Jersey. Although I had driven down earlier today, I had also planned to drive to Kesher Israel from the hotel. However, I ended up using a taxi. Thank goodness for those little apps on our phones. What would we now do without them? Anyway, no one likes to witness devastation or destruction. But when you see it, you begin to realize the power of hatred."

He wasn't sure that was an opening anybody in their wildest dreams expected to hear.

"Lately, we seem to be witnessing a fair share of turmoil – wars, unrest, violence, skirmishes, riots. I'm not keeping score by any measure, but every day something new seems to be reported. When you see this amount of destruction, you wonder, I know I wonder, what's the rationale? It's all so senseless. It's such a waste. At some point, you have to come to the realization we live in a time of unadulterated and broad-scale hatred. We can take this opportunity to study the human condition. Specifically, a condition of looking into the heart of darkness, into the abyss of what happens when a person gets consumed with hate." Eli was also thinking about the knife left in his tire.

"Whenever hatred takes over and consumes a person or even a group of individuals, the unfolding and terrible devastation can be worse than any cancer. Hatred is complete insanity. I'm not just referring to anti-Semitism. Blacks, Asians, police, gays, and whole countries are all susceptible to becoming a target of hatred. For us, we saw in Nazi Europe when hatred spawns, it ceases to have to make any sense. The perpetrated atrocities and how they are perpetrated can only leave us dumbfounded. The sadism and mutilation that goes on. Every time, we see perpetrators celebrating we can only conclude their tremendous hatred has overtaken the soul. It's reasonable to think we are all capable of holding a grievance. We can even have many complaints. But when it turns into hatred." He paused. Whether for effect or to recenter himself, it lasted for what felt like a minute.

"That's the nuance. When someone needs to express their hatred, they'll invariably do it without considering the consequences. We can witness what hatred does to a human being, to the human soul. It's like a demonic force taking possession of a body. A person consumed by hate is not inhibited. They can perform all kinds of heinous and unspeakable things. Even if those things end up hurting themselves and their own families. On a subtle level, it's nothing less than bewildering."

He looked around the congregation to gauge interest. The other rabbi just gave an expression of someone who had just allowed Pandora's Box to be opened. Eli decided to keep going.

"We see people who enter into litigation. People will spend enormous sums of money on attorneys for no other purpose than to get even with someone. And why? Just to win! That's not about justice. That's not about right or wrong. It's about vengeance; it's about bringing forth hatred. The senselessness of it. Now, by contrast, the diametric opposite of hate is love. But it turns out hate can teach us more about love than love can teach us about love. This is because love does the exact opposite of hate. Love is nurturing, validating, and bringing out the best within us and others while hatred destroys. Hatred breaks things apart, beginning with your own inner self. Love connects, unites, fuses, and synergizes. So, of course, the antidote to hate is love. But it's not so simple. When a person is in the throes of acting on something they really hate, you can't just say to them, 'Hey!' That's because they won't see the problem. They think their actions are justified. But for us who can observe, hate teaches us to embrace each other and our loved ones with even more passion than ever before. We know this because of the destruction we see hate leave in its wake."

Even while speaking, he could sense the congregants being engrossed by what was being said. He wasn't observing anyone fidgeting and moving around in their seat, itching to find the exit.

"When you've been a victim, when you've been subject to hatred, and you've been hurt by people who've hated you, the temptation is to fight fire with fire. But no. We must dig deeper into our spirits to realize we must not become defined by other people's hatred. I'm telling you right now, I won't become defined by someone who hates me. I will be defined by those who love me. I will be defined by my higher purpose. My divine being. My divine self. But this all takes work. It takes effort. The biggest *mitzvah*, potentially the biggest commandment we can find in the Torah, is to love others as you love yourself."

Eli knew it was time to bring his ad-hoc digestible to a close.

"We have before us a tremendous opportunity, both on a microcosm and macrocosm level, to look at ourselves, to look at the better angels within us, but also to the possible demons that have the potential to consume us. When we work on ourselves in our own personal way, it has an effect. We know from modern physics how something in one place can impact something else elsewhere. Physicists call this the Butterfly Effect. So, there is something we all can do. When you repair even a subtle form of dislike or hatred for something else, you are, in fact, correcting something. Affecting the vibes, the environment, and the very energy of this world. It all comes down to energy. And hateful energy always becomes destructive. It breaks things apart. Loving energy unites. So, it's no surprise the prophet Isaiah said, and I'm paraphrasing here, 'There will no longer be evil, and we will no longer see destruction,' when he spoke about the future. The Hebrew word for peace is *shalom*. But *shalom* doesn't just mean the absence of war, just like love doesn't mean the absence of hate. *Shalom* means complete wholesomeness. It's an entity of its own reality, of its own love. May we embrace filling the world with divine knowledge, eradicating all evil, destruction, divisiveness, devastation, and ultimately, all forms of hatred. May we channel and harness the energies within us toward a passionate revolution, a spiritual revolution where we have diversity and where there is harmony within that diversity. May we all see it and experience it in a revealed fashion. *Shalom.*"

OTTO AND ELI

"I MUST SAY, THE AIR WAS BEAUTIFUL OUTSIDE THIS MORNING. Very fresh. For some reason, I woke a little earlier than usual, so I took the opportunity to go out for a gentle run while my seasoned knees are still game! I wasn't expecting to see so many people running around The Mall. It's always pleasant to run with the crowd, so to speak!" Eli said. He withheld mentioning the incident from the prior evening as a potential cause for his early arousal.

"I wish I could, but my knees have been out of season for some time now," Otto said.

"I was just past the Lincoln Memorial when I caught a serendipitous moment. Two individuals brushed paths, and in that delicate exchange, there was an unintended stumble. I halted in my tracks to offer assistance. The poor woman had a twisted ankle. I extended a steadying hand to aid her transition toward respite and one of the ornate benches around that part of The Mall. With the extra police on duty today, I was able to alert an officer to the situation. She radioed for a medic, and one showed up in less than two minutes. I was reminded of the curious dance between fortune and misfortune," Eli said.

"Unfortunately, life is fraught with challenges and difficulties, even one as trivial as an engine malfunction."

"That old conundrum of celebration, joy, happiness, beautiful events, and experiences, countered with the distresses of anxiety, pain, and suffering."

"It's probably the most asked question I've experienced during my time in shepherding souls. 'How can a good God allow bad things to happen?' A line of inquiry as ancient as faith itself; the nature of the question clings to the fabric of contemplation with unyielding tenacity. As we speak, Geronimo's purposeful stride is on his way here, and today's anniversary is a sullen reminder of the abundance of God's child harboring lost souls," Otto said.

"For these precise reasons, some will completely dismiss the notion that God even exists."

"Those are also the souls seeking justice over faith. But when ominous clouds strike, and you have pain, or you see pain, when you bear witness to a loss, a trauma, an anxiety, it's easy for this question to pop up, emerging without effort, like a whispered secret carried on the wind."

"Pop-up is a little dismissive, don't you think?" Eli asked.

"You're right. Let me rephrase. These questions plague us."

"When you think about it, it's unsurprising. Most people start life being told that God is the Creator, that we trust in

God, the Creator of goodness. We grow up with the illusion that only good shall befall us. So, it's understandable when we hear, 'Why is God allowing this to happen to me?' They blame God," Eli said.

"Even Moses, in his great leadership, voiced blame. He said, 'Why, Lord, why have you brought trouble on this people?' Regrettably, it's woven into our human nature to lay blame when seeking explanations. A child who looks to her parents for protection, still inquires 'why' when hardship enters their world."

"I think we can agree that it's a completely legitimate question, and yet the answer is far more complicated than the question itself," Eli said.

"If for no other reason that it is God who put us here on Earth, and not the other way around, that we put God in heaven. We are right to ask such questions, but it's our job to help our flocks understand the Creator. Do you ever do *The Times* crossword?"

"I usually only have time on Sunday," Eli said. He chuckled a little.

"Yesterday, one of their clues was something like, 'A simmering stew, he could take the heat turned up from the cook's concoction without losing his savory patience.'"

"Job," Eli said.

"Exactly. I can see we're going to get along just fine. As the classic sufferer, when Job asks the question, and I'm paraphrasing here, 'Why is there pain and suffering in this world? You're a good God.' One of God's responses is, 'Were you there when I created heaven and Earth? Why do you ask me such a question?'"

"A'foe hi'e'ta b'as'di a'retz ha'ged im ya'da'ta be'nah. 'Where were you when I laid the foundations of the Earth? Declare if you have the understanding,'" Eli said.

"Excellent. Job thirty-eight, four. Good, good. So, God is anchoring our understanding of how we could comprehend something that is bad if we weren't part of the master plan in the creation process. 'Were you there?' God is rhetorically asking. He knows all of us have to answer 'No.' God probes why we ask about death – why we have an end, but why we don't ask about life – why we have a beginning. He further asks why we ask about pain, yet we don't ask about joy. It becomes painfully clear. Anything we consider bad and anything we think is good are inextricably bound together."

"Yes, our questions are generally asked when we are not comfortable and when we are not happy. For some reason, we take for granted when things are good, which is a testimony to a good God," Eli said.

"Why do we assume things will never be bad? Good Lord, forbid. Something within us, beating inside of us, assumed goodness will ultimately prevail."

"Yes, some people have been hurt, some deeply, and therefore, they've lowered their expectations to the point where they always expect the worst. But that's not how we're born," Eli said.

"Children have a natural exuberance, a natural joy, and optimism. So, when speaking to Job, God essentially explains life's mysteries. If you were never born, you'd never die. If you didn't have life, you wouldn't have pain. The question, of course, is, can there be a life without pain? Which connects us to the question, why is there life in the first place?"

"May I take your order, Rabbi?" the waitress asked.

"Challah toast, please," Eli said.

"Any protein with that?"

"Butter."

"Butter?"

"Butter."

"That's not very high in protein."

"I'll try and do better at lunch," he said.

"I'll have that for you right away." The waitress headed back toward the kitchen door.

"It's also a question that has been attempted outside of the Bible. Throughout history, great men and women have tried to deal with the question. We all have dealt with this very question at some point. Nobody is immune from pain, suffering, and loss, and we must recognize that on anniversaries such as today – eight children died – we see tragedies far, far beyond the pale."

"So, a child born, for no reason of their own, comes into the world in a way that will be challenging to them and the family. So, big questions can be asked when we see these things."

"I would say the classic answer we often hear is, in fact, silence."

"In Leviticus, when Aaron's children died prematurely

before God, in chapter ten, verse three, we are told, 'And Aaron held his peace.'"

"Also, when the Romans barbarically killed the ten Jewish martyrs, the Midrash *Eleh Ezkerah* says that God's reply as to why this happened was not a concise answer. God said, 'This is the Torah, and this is its reward.' In other words, God didn't prevent the ten greatest intellects of the Jewish people from being massacred. The Lord's basic response was, 'Be silent.' Why? Because silence isn't an escape. Silence is an answer."

"I agree. Silence can be a prudent answer. It's saying that no matter what reason you give, the most brilliant human mind cannot speak to a bleeding heart. It's acknowledging and validating the very unfathomable experience of pain and suffering."

"Exactly, when someone is suffering, they're not looking for explanations and excuses. People may ask why, but what are we going to say? Are we going to try and provide an excuse? Are we going to try and explain why the Holocaust happened? Are we going to explain to a mother why her child was killed in a car accident? Heaven forbid! What people need is empathy. Perhaps, just to hold their hand. If nothing else, it'll let them know, 'I'm with you.' A great rebbe once said to a person suffering a tragedy, 'I don't have answers for you, but I can cry with you.'"

"We shouldn't underestimate the power of such a simple message. In reality, we are acknowledging and recognizing that we're dealing with an abyss no human being is in a position to fathom. None of us, if we are being honest, can wrap our heads around the issue. It's why faith is so important."

"People aren't always looking for explanations. They are looking for strength. Strength, not silence. And what does strength mean? It means we don't ask why."

"Or another way to understand this is when we ask, 'What are we going to do about it?' 'How am I going to get through this?' 'How am I going to rebuild?' 'How am I going to justify it?' I don't mean justify as a justification, but justify the pain by transforming it into something positive. Now that is an answer."

"This is a tough one for me. It's difficult not to be able to explain why God allows negative things to happen. We can try to rationalize the dynamics of how God put in place a system, a system where things are allowed to occur – but why? In each case, we can always say God should have done it differently."

"The first step we have to acknowledge is that pain is not meant to be justified. It's not meant to be explained away. It's meant to be absorbed. The only way out is through. It's meant to figure out how to build greater strengths. That's what we're seeking. So, in such a context, when a person is in the emotional throes of pain, they're not looking for answers. Answers won't help. The heart will help. Empathy will help."

"You may want to sit down and discuss it philosophically once the emotions are not as intense."

"Agreed. But let's first acknowledge and allow ourselves to be silent in the pain. Silence is more powerful than sound. Silence is more powerful than answers. Indeed, even after great tragedy, we see our parishioners go on to grow and build successful lives. And, no doubt, what they created for themselves could never have been built without the pain of grief."

"Negative things, grief, sadness, these are all just energy. I like to call it inverted energy, something like a black hole millions of light years from here."

"Precisely. A black hole has a gravitational pull so intense that it doesn't allow light to escape – precisely like pain. As you say, there's tremendous energy. So how do we tap into it?"

"By transforming it into something."

"I remember when my father passed away. It was all very traumatic at the time – deep, deep grief. It was one of the most traumatic events in my life. But I would say I've led a blessed life and I thank God with gratitude. I've seen people suffering in ways I simply can't begin to imagine. But at the same time, the grief I experienced, the catharsis, the healing, was when I channeled my father into how I engage with others. I would love to be sitting here with my father, embracing him and having him be part of our conversation, but to say that his passing was just grief, a dead end, absolutely not. The grief was channeled. Returning to Job's story, we recognize there's a deeper story to life. Would we prefer not to have a life? Some may say 'perhaps' as a reflection of a particular situation they find themselves in. But, building a better world in partnership with God is a purpose given to us in having free will."

"The same free will gives people the ability to choose to do good or to hurt someone."

"It's all part of the process. The goal is not hurt. The goal is to choose. But to choose requires options. You could say, 'Okay, fine, human beings hurt one another, but what about God allowing tragedy to happen?'"

"Here's your toasted challah and butter," the waitress said. She turned to face Otto. "Your eggs will be out in a moment. The kitchen's very busy, and your soft-boiled eggs became hard-boiled. So, the chef's working on doing them over. You shouldn't have to wait too long."

Otto and Eli looked around the restaurant. Except for one other patron, the dining room was empty.

"Busy?" Otto asked.

"We have a lot of orders for room service this morning," the waitress said.

"Thank you," Otto said. "All's good."

The waitress left.

"To create existence, an independent consciousness like ourselves, God needed to conceal his divine presence," Otto said. "So long as the divine presence is present, we have the divine good. But, there's no room for independence. I tell my newly married parishioners to think of it as a parent watching a child take its first steps. The child will inevitably fall unless the parent holds on. No parent wants to hold a child forever. Parents want their children to walk. It's not an act of compassion to hold your child. You don't want the child to be hurt or upset, but you restrain your instinct to hold so the child will learn to toddle around on its own. You need to create an independent space. God had to let us become our own entity. Otherwise, we're just puppets and robots fulfilling God's goodness. There would be no purpose to existence."

"Well put," Eli said. "The very purpose of existence paves the way for independence, and independence allows room for hurt."

"A classic example is a parent hiding from a child to elicit the child's ingenuity to find the parent. But if a parent hides themselves too well, the child might give up looking. The concealment was not to evade. The concealment was to elicit the child's intelligence. Essentially, all negative things in life result from misunderstood concealment."

"Yes, we don't understand why God is concealed, so it's all too easy to go off on our own. Within existence, we can do things inconsistently and not aligned with the divine goodness. Therefore, we have tragedy, loss, pain, and suffering."

"But you wouldn't use that to explain why something bad is happening. Your reasoning simply explains the dynamics of independence as a means to how or why something bad can happen."

"If you shelter your child and keep them at home, there may be some protection, but the child will never become independent. The child will never spread his or her wings. Part and parcel of a life of purpose and a life of choice is the ability for something untoward to happen."

"Thus, we have the purpose of concealment, which is to reveal. That's why a tremendous amount of energy lies

THE FLAT TIRE

within grief, sadness, and loss. When we see through the concealment, we can understand the concealment, and we see its purpose. We can tap into it. Anyone who's come to any real level of growth, sees how setbacks have propelled them forward."

"We need to be wise and not get consumed with our pains. Yes, there's a time to cry, a time to grieve, and there's a time to let all of the anguish seep through. Finding a way to channel the resulting energy is key to enabling tremendous positive growth. Still, in truth – we don't know the final answer. It has to be silence. But what can we do about it?"

A female voice came from the side of the table. It was not the server. "Namaste. I'm Doctor Linda Herzog." She extended her hand toward Otto.

"Cardinal Otto LaMacchia," he said. *Apparently, she wants titles,* he thought. He shook her hand. "And this is Rabbi Rahabi."

Linda and Eli shook hands.

"I told the host I could find my way to this table – not difficult to navigate a restaurant where only one table has two people. I understand we'll have the pleasure of meeting Ms. Moytoy shortly."

"Oh, please have a seat, Doctor Herzog," the Cardinal said.

"Please, call me Linda," she said. "Silly of me to use my title in the introduction. Too many seminars, I guess." She was attired in faded, button-fly blue jeans. A thick, brown leather belt with a silver buckle showed its wear. On her feet, she wore elk-colored hiking boots with mountain-red laces. Her short-sleeved knit summer-time sweater was made with textural mohair and featured subtle tonal stripes with a relaxed silhouette. Over her shoulder, she carried a small black crocheted bag, which looked like it wasn't holding much of anything. Her gray hair was worn up, and she had not applied any noticeable makeup. A thin red cotton bracelet encircled her left wrist. She looked at odds with her two gentlemen companions in tailored suits. While Otto wore a tie and a pocket square; Eli sported an open collar.

"I'm Otto," he said. "This is Eli."

"Eli. How interesting. I met an Ellie while I was making my way to D.C."

"Here's your soft-boiled eggs and toast, Cardinal," the waitress said. She looked at Linda. "Would you care for a menu, Doctor?"

"No, thank you. Black coffee and a toasted croissant if you have?"

"Right away. Any juice?"

"No, thank you." Turning back to her breakfast companions, she began, "You probably didn't have any issues coming in. I left Bozeman, Montana, on the eighth to get here. It's out west near the Rockies. I had been visiting a friend. With everyone worried about their carbon footprint – you're worried about that, right? – I decided to hitchhike. I thought it would be fun. Something different. Haven't tried it since my undergraduate days. And we won't discuss how long that's been!"

THE FLAT TIRE

She wasn't pausing long enough to take a breath. Otto and Eli let her take center stage while they began to nibble at their breakfasts.

"My first ride was in Bozeman, but they could only take me as far as Billings. Her name was Ellie. Just like yours. How funny. Who'd have thought? Anyway, the darling was a queer artist trying to find her way and fit in. I bought her a cup of coffee to go at Uncle Bunny's as a thank you. Then, I got a ride from Carlos. Very handsome, but I've never been so scared. He was quite the philanderer. I felt very intimidated and scared if I'm honest. Fortunately, I was able to evade him in Bismarck before anything could happen. He was going through a massive midlife crisis. He was obviously using his jacked-up truck as a phallic extension of himself."

Linda had no compunction about adjusting her vocabulary in front of the two clerics.

"I got a very nice ride to Chicago from a trucker named Rusty, where I met a wonderfully nice lesbian named Alex. She got me as far as Sylvania. That's in Ohio. Next was a set of demure twins. They were reticent."

"Your coffee and croissant, Doctor," the waitress said.

"Thank you, I appreciate your contributions, valued ally," Linda said. She noticed how young, very young the girl looked. And those eyes – the girl had mesmerizing green eyes and dark black eyebrows – appeared to holler, "Yeah, that's right. Gawk all you want. You know you want me!"

"Where was I? Oh yes, that's right. So, yesterday morning after I checked out, a man was in the parking lot looking at his flat tire. He looked like, 'Why do bad things always happen to me?' He looked helpless and hopeless. I brushed him aside and changed the flat. You're both lucky you didn't have to deal with flat tires on your trip here! That car had some tight lug nuts, let me tell you. I had to jump on the tire iron to get them to move. Anyway, it turned out he was headed to D.C., so I found my final ride and got here in plenty of time. It's so nice out today, don't you think? So, how's your day?"

Finally, Linda took a moment to inhale and sip her coffee. "I hope I wasn't interrupting anything?"

OTTO, ELI, AND LINDA

"A RABBI," LINDA SAID. "I WAS RAISED IN A JEWISH household, although our identity was labeled as the intriguing blend, 'Jewish-Italian.' I'm not sure when they felt the need to add the Italian. It must have been early in their marriage when they chose to temper the resonance of Jewishness. Adding Italian allowed the illusion of intermingled hues of Catholic blood. They thought it would provide an element of safety against the turbulent winds of prejudice and anti-Semitic backlash. When I was in high school, they just referred to the family as being Italian – though our lineage is more Hungarian than Italian."

"Yes. A rabbi," Eli said.

"Where's your congregation?"

"Jersey," Eli said.

"Have you been a rabbi your entire adult life?"

"Not always, no."

"What caused you to have your come to Jesus moment?" she asked. "So, to speak."

"I led a life of crime," Eli said without drama. "And after seven years in a New York State penitentiary, I chose this road to follow."

"You're joking," Otto said. "Come now. Seriously, when did you have your come to Jesus moment?" He looked at Linda and winked.

Eli told Linda and Otto how naïve he'd been in his younger days and how he lost everything during his former career when reckless greed took over. His prison sentence for insider trading left him years alone with his cot and his regrets. But it also gave him time to rediscover his Jewish heritage, and studying the Torah became his salvation.

By the time of his parole, he was a changed man. He'd discovered meaning, not in material things but in service and community. Once ordained, he turned his mission into guiding others in his newfound light. Though he could not undo his crimes, as a rabbi, he hoped to steer those who would hear his message toward righteousness and redemption.

The seven years in a medium-security prison delivered a harsh wake-up call after his privileged upbringing and Wall Street success. Gone were the luxuries and sense of control to which he was accustomed. Back then, he was twisted enough to think his flaunted luxury was a right. But once he was incarcerated, the emptiness of his ambitious striving was immediate.

Initially, he struggled to adapt to the monotonous

routine in his new home, the prison. Assigned a small, sparse cell, he was confined for long stretches each day. More broadly speaking, privacy was nonexistent, and distractions were constant. The guards yelled. Inmates fought. Televisions were played with the volume turned up all the way. Finding the mental space for spiritual reflection amidst the chaos was challenging.

During the limited library hours, Ezekiel dove into Torah and Talmud studies. Distracted by the noises and cramped conditions, he persevered. He gained an appreciation for the etymology of the ancient texts and compiled a manuscript of teachings to guide his redemption.

"But, going back to your comment on lineage with a Hungarian and Italian background," Eli said wishing to change the subject. "My family describes our lineage as from the Middle East and India."

Otto's ears pricked up.

"I took a DNA test some years ago, and it seems somebody in the family strayed. Within those molecular echoes resided a tale of wanderings, a trace of footsteps divergent from the expected path. There was quite a bit of DNA from somewhere I didn't expect. My given name, Eli, is short for Ezekiel. My namesake settled in southwest India in a city called Kochi during the sixteen hundreds or thereabouts. Who knew, right? Jews in India! Apparently, there's a synagogue originally built during the fifteen-sixties by a group of the city's prosperous Jewish traders. There were other synagogues, even earlier ones, but they've all been lost to time. The original settlers would have been Sephardic and exiled during the Spanish Inquisition. One of Ezekiel's descendants, also named Ezekiel, worked for the Dutch East India Company in the seventeen hundreds. With deft hands and visionary zeal, he helped refurbish the synagogue and added a forty-five-foot-tall clock tower. He also added a blue and white tile floor that still exists today. At one point, a smallpox outbreak killed off many of the local population. I think that's when the bulk of the intermarriage, or affairs, took place, which accounts for my Indian heritage all forgotten by time but remembered by DNA. So, I'm Jewish-American-Syrian-Dutch-Indian or something like that. A true mutt!" Eli smiled.

"Fascinating. I've been to Kochi," Otto said. "I'll tell you about it a little later. Keep going with your story. When does the hardened criminal come into the picture?"

"After I completed my master's with honors, I was bombarded with offers to join various traders. Mecca came calling, more commonly known as Wall Street. And there I went. Young, full of energy. Everything and everybody was measured. My grade point average exceeded four-point-oh. I got straight A's plus extra credit. I received recognition from the Academic Awards Committee. I excelled, and I let my achievements go to my head. I didn't want to stop being measured as the standout. I wanted all of Wall Street to declare me number one. I needed to bring in a lot of money – a shit load. Pardon my French. I let my ego get in the way. My life focused on one thing, money. Anything that didn't drive revenue got moved off the stove. I began to cheat. I started using my contacts to trade on inside information – a habit as addictive as opioids."

Linda and Otto were engaged, their mouths gaping wider with each sentence.

"The Securities and Exchange Commission got wind of what was happening. They alerted the FBI, who, I must say, were very thorough with their investigation. They, in turn, brought the federal trial court, the Southern District of New York, into the frame. I was buying shares under various pseudonyms and aliases with different accounts; I thought I was being careful." He paused.

"Go on," Otto said.

"Unbeknownst to me, my firm had installed some sophisticated software systems. They analyzed trading data in real-time to detect anomalous patterns, volume spikes, and rapid price changes. Everything was in place before I joined. I triggered a number of alerts. When approached, my firm shared the information with the SEC. From there, I was crispier than this toast."

"Oh, my goodness," Linda said.

"The authorities acted in unison to unravel my labyrinthine web of deceit. Their investigative prowess uncovered my intricate shenanigans and traced everything back to the source – me. They were quite meticulous in reconstructing every trade. The case was ironclad. My sentence was thirty-two years. With good behavior, I served the seven I had told you about." Eli had fallen back into embellishing his prison story.

"Now I can appreciate how you had your coming to Jesus crisis!" Linda said.

"I served my term nestled in New York State's picturesque Catskills. In my wildest hopes, I prayed for one of the aging resort hotels with a pool and a dance hall. When I got there, I found myself inhabiting an altogether different type of enclave. I was in the embrace of the Otisville Federal Correctional Institution, Cell one-fifty-six. The warden referred to each cell as 'inmate housing.' For seven years, I stayed in my house. It came fully furnished: a cot and a stainless-steel latrine with no seat. There was no closet. There was no bone China. I didn't need them anyway."

"Well, at least you've got a sense of humor," Linda said.

"The prison still holds a reputation as one of New York's more hospitable federal corrections institutions. The attraction of Jewish studies beckoned, and I followed. I found myself unearthing my Jewish heritage; I could even get kosher meals. My curiosity became a consuming blaze as I delved deeper into the knowledge embedded in ancient texts. Upon my release, the trajectory of my life pivoted toward a *Yeshiva*. Upon being ordained, the practical chapters of my narrative unfurled. I zealously entered into internships within congregations, hospitals, and even correctional facilities. It was a phase of immersion, a time when theory and faith coalesced with practice, refining my understanding of human connection and spiritual guidance. These were the years of forging connections, of illuminating paths for those navigating moments of

THE FLAT TIRE

darkness. And then, the culmination of my odyssey arrived. In the heart of a neglected corner of New Jersey, where hope seemed to have worn thin, I was given my own *shul*. Amidst the echoes of history and the whispered aspirations of a small and thinning congregation, I found my purpose – to nurture the souls entrusted to my care became my *raison d'être*. That's the gist of my story, a journey through the corridors of incarceration, reawakening through study, and the metamorphosis into a spiritual guide. From the confinements of a prison to the expanses of a congregation, my path has been one of rediscovery, renewal, and resilience."

"Did you get to keep any of the money?" Linda asked.

"Not a cent. I didn't get to keep anything. All I have now is my small salary and the little bit extra I make from the tiny lessons I post – the ByteSize social media app calls them edibles."

"Fascinating! I thought your name sounded familiar," Otto said. "Some of my younger fathers tell me I should get with the times and create some of those. In fact, I think they may have shown me one of yours!"

"How about you, Otto? Have you had a wayward past, or have you always been a man of the cloth?" Linda asked.

"I don't believe I would have had my consistory if I'd had Eli's checkered past. Forgive me. I meant no offense, Eli."

"None taken."

"Actually, I only recently became a cardinal. You may have seen in the news that Nashville became a See earlier this year. I am fortunate enough to serve as the first cardinal. But, before I forget, I want to discuss our Kochi connection."

"Go for it," Eli said.

Otto began. In his early days as "the Fresh Priest of Bel Air," a name he'd acquired during the early weeks of his first assignment to a Catholic Church nestled in the heart of Bel Air in Los Angeles, he mingled with many of the university students from UCLA who attended services. He uncovered his love for connecting with his brothers and sisters from different backgrounds. He gained an understanding of the profound significance of building a network of relationships transcending geographical borders within his faith. For him, an opportunity to venture somewhere new was not about seeing the world but a chance to connect with its people.

Whenever whispers of a distant land reached his ears, his heart would sing with anticipation. His humble priestly duties never confined him; rather, they propelled him to step beyond the confines of one church and immerse himself in the lives of other parishioners. A journey was never defined by tourist attractions but by the faces of the parishioners – his brothers and sisters and the stories they shared. He reveled in the camaraderie he encountered from a shared devotion to the Lord Jesus Christ. In those moments, the web of his network grew stronger, uniting connections transcending time and distance.

Bishops and even the occasional cardinal graced Otto's path. He would humbly engage in conversations ranging from theology to shared laughter. He discovered that titles faded in the presence of shared humanity, and the bonds forged through shared faith were unbreakable. One connection shone brighter among the many faces, a fellow priest from Kerala state in India, the city of Kochi. The city was introduced to Christianity by Saint Thomas – the one everyone called "Doubting Thomas." Otto associated the connection with a ray of divine light. Their shared passion for service and unyielding dedication to faith and serving the local community bound them together in a unique way. The years flowed like rivers, but the connection remained.

The priest from Kochi ascended the spiritual ranks, becoming a cardinal. Their friendship remained untouched by the robes, the title, and the trappings of power. Otto and the cardinal exchanged letters and emails full of news as well as the essence of their friendship. Through emails spanning continents, they shared laughter, offered solace, and celebrated each other's triumphs.

Otto's journeys continued, each a testament to his unwavering commitment to fostering relationships. The world became a scrapbook of faces and stories, each thread interwoven with his own. He stood as a living testament to the power of human connection – a priest who understood how the essence of faith extended beyond rituals and creeds. Moreover, he understood the power a vast network can yield.

"There was an outbreak of something medical. I won't mention with what as we're eating," he said. "The situation presented an opportunity to help a priest lead an early morning Mass. The aura of the situation resonated within me. There was a certain *je ne sais quoi*, a unique, monumental blend of spirit. The congregation gathered in the majesty of the majestic church to partake in the Eucharist. The morning sun painted the horizon in hues of amber and gold, casting a fresh glow over the gathering. People from many countries had assembled to listen to the words from the lips of two messengers of God. We shared a message of unity, how the strands of belief and shared commonality as human beings can bind humanity together despite differences in culture, language, and geography of birth."

"Sounds fascinating," Linda said.

"I've not been there for decades, but I was told they had found a Mexican priest who could communicate in all the languages spoken at that church: Telegu, Hindi, Malayalam, English, and even Mandarin. So many languages, I can't even remember them all."

"Must have been a fascinating person!" Linda said.

"Anyway, during this particular service, the air vibrated with a sense of harmony. That's the best way I can describe the experience. Our voices intertwined like melodies in an opus of devotion. Our message of kindling the lamp of hope even in the darkest of hours and how finding profound connections can occur through our capacity for boundless, unconditional love served as a means to comprehend the essence of existence. The sense of unity was palpable. It touched the hearts of the congregation, stirring dormant emotions waiting for the right catalyst. At the conclusion, the congregation left with spirits uplifted and hearts brimming with a renewed sense of purpose. Inspired by the profound impact of the service, people felt compelled to contribute more than they normally would. A sense of awe swept through the church when the collection was counted. The donations received were almost double the typical amount."

"Good for you," Linda said.

"We were giddy ourselves from the spiritual experience, and we embarked on an impromptu journey through the streets of Kochi. We rode around the city on a rickshaw. The vessel allowed us to experience the sights, honking horns, and smells of the city firsthand. We even drove by your Paradesi Synagogue, Eli, whose majestic clock tower stood tall against the sky. I recall gazing upon its antique architecture and feeling a deep respect for the history and faith it represented. Kochi was a wonderful experience, and because of what the place means to me, I am so happy we share it in common."

Otto wasn't schmoozing. He was networking with Eli. Feeling a little left out from the male bonding, Linda threw a question into the mix more as a knee-jerk reaction than out of curiosity.

"Aren't you losing members in your new See because of the Pope's last missive on morality? I think in this day and age, your parishioners won't buy his stand on birth control, let alone sex education and divorce. Do you think he'll ever maneuver to give some latitude on these issues?" she asked.

That's a great question. Let me make a mental note to remember it just in case, Otto thought. "The times are changing," he said. "I gave a speech at my consistory dinner on change from a secular point of view. I'm sure the Holy Father will always do what is best."

Otto turned the conversation to focus on Linda to deflect any further probing. "Tell me, Doctor, what's your story outside of hitchhiking? Are you a medical doctor?" *You're not coming across as a doctor of theology,* he thought.

"I have two doctorates in philosophy – one from Cambridge and my second from Berkeley. But tell me, Cardinal, and you too, Rabbi, I am curious, being the only biological female at the table, how do you reconcile that God formed man from the dust of the ground but used one of man's ribs to make a woman. I can draw your attention to the distinction between something 'formed' and something 'made.' The distinction holds a depth of meaning that transcends mere semantics. I could argue that being 'made' carries a unique significance, suggesting a connection to a higher form of creation and a potential indication of superiority. On the contrary, when something is 'formed,' it implies a process of shaping and molding from existing materials. When God 'formed' man, it suggests a careful arrangement akin to an artist molding clay with intention and artistry. We could say it signifies a personal touch and even a purposeful design. On the other hand, when something is 'made,' it signifies an ardent act of creation initiated from a higher level of consciousness and authority. Such an act implies a deliberate decision to bring something into existence from a source that transcends the immediate materials at hand. Furthermore, that a woman was 'made' suggests divine agency, elevating the creation above the sum of its parts. I suggest, gentlemen, that being 'made' is indeed an indication of superiority."

"The distinction you are trying to draw does not necessarily imply a hierarchy of superiority," Otto said. "Instead, the texts can simply be interpreted as highlighting the unique roles and attributes of both men and women without assigning one as inherently better than the other. Taken in context, both words speak to the intentionality and purpose behind their creation rather than indicating a hierarchy of value. Whether through forming or making, both are a reflection of God's intention to create beings that complement and support one another to form a harmonious partnership."

"I would emphasize the concept of balance and the interconnectedness of masculine and feminine energies within every individual," Eli said. "According to Kabbalistic teachings, the idea that all men have a feminine side and all women have a masculine side is rooted in understanding the *sefirot*, the ten attributes emanating from the Divine. The idea of having a masculine side within women and a feminine side within men highlights the dynamic nature of the soul and its journey toward spiritual wholeness. We are all made in the image of God, *B'tzelem Elohim*, which encompasses both masculine and feminine attributes. This concept reinforces the idea that each person embodies a balance of energies reflecting the divine blueprint."

"I can see how such thoughts may have contributed to your agnostic beliefs," Otto said.

"Eli, do you see gender as a performative act?" Linda asked.

"Pardon me for interrupting," Jabari said. "I've just received a message from our concierge desk. Ms. Moytoy sends her apologies and won't be able to join you for breakfast this morning. Apparently, a double whammy. First, she had a flat tire on her way into the office, and then she received an unexpected call from the Chairman of the House Ways and Means Committee. She's asked if you'd kindly meet one of her interns in the hotel lobby at 10:00 a.m. You'll be escorted across the street to the law office. The intern will navigate building security and get your badges for the day. May I get anybody some more coffee or juice? Will you please excuse me for one moment? I can see another guest at the reception desk."

A minute later, Jabari came back to the table. A man trailed behind. "This gentleman is with you," he said.

"Thank you," Martin said. He extended his hand toward Linda and introduced himself.

"Doctor Herzog, I'm Imam Martin."

"First or last name?" she asked.

"Mononymous," he said, "but hardly on the level of Topol, Pelé, or Beyoncé."

"Pleasure," she said.

The others introduced themselves in turn.

"Cardinal Otto LaMacchia. A pleasure."

"Rabbi Eli Rahabi. Please sit. Welcome."

CAMILA

CAMILA GRACEFULLY ENTERED THE KITCHEN, LEAVING THE dining room guests to their various conversations. Her presence on the morning's wait staff provided a seamless addition to the coordinated chaos associated with hotel staff in satisfying the discriminating needs of a discerning clientele. Normally, the torchbearer of evening culinary delights was the award-winning chef who would coordinate the culinary wonders on any other day with a team of skilled line cooks, prep cooks, and a sous chef. Night after night, her talents lead the band to dance to her rhythm. However, this morning was different. The chef had donned an unfamiliar hat, stepping in for the morning-shift chef who had been given a few days off to stand vigil by a sick relative in hospice.

The chef took a moment to inquire about the clockwork of events. In her usual tone of camaraderie, she asked Camila about her morning tardiness. It was the first time she'd been late for work since beginning her job two months prior. Camila's small, two-door Subaru had experienced some difficulties while en route to her local metro station.

With genuine concern etched on her features, the chef leaned in, a culinary wiz pausing to listen. Camila's narrative unfolded the woes of a flat tire, an unexpected hurdle in her journey to the New Carrollton Metro Station in Maryland. Her tone carried the weight of the morning's unforeseen adversity. Mouthwatering aromas floated past while she described her ordeal in great detail.

In the heat of the morning rush, she had guided her modest, underpowered econobox to miss some falling debris from a passing pickup truck. Her reaction set her on a new course, one aligned to smack the jaws of a lurking pothole squarely in the mouth. The Subaru's MacPherson strut, designed to slash noise, vibration, and harshness, released a mighty crunch as the tire blew. Reverberations shot along the steering column to the steering wheel and into her small frame. Holding on for dear life, she fought hard to maintain control of the vehicle and guided it to the hard shoulder, where she turned off the ignition. She'd always been brought up to be self-sufficient, so she set about doing what she needed to do. She got out of the car and examined the carnage. Beelining for the trunk, she pulled out the spare donut and changed the tire. Once replaced, she completed her journey to the parking lot at the train station and boarded the Orange Line train to the bustling artery of the Metro Center. Once there, she took a brisk, four-tenths-of-a-mile walk to the hotel. The staff had a designated locker room on the ground floor with separate facilities for men and women. She took a deep breath, washed her hands and face, rearranged her hair, and changed into her work uniform.

An understanding shake of the head followed the chef's sympathetic gaze. "And where's your name badge?" the chef asked.

"Gosh, darn. I must've left it in the car."

Although new to waitressing, Camila was freshly adorned with the laurels of academic achievement. Emerging from the legendary auditoriums of Johns Hopkins University, she clutched her master's degree in Public Health as a testament to her scholastic dedication. Her undergraduate degree in Environmental Biology was received from Georgetown University. In the wake of these academic triumphs, she stood at a crossroads, a valedictorian at the intersection of opportunity and respite. The prestigious Johns Hopkins beckoned her to pursue a Doctor of Public Health, an accolade offering the promise of following a path to serve – the same path her parents had trod. Yet, beneath the robes of academic achievement, she recognized the need for an ephemeral hiatus – a moment to exhale, a chance for some space to inhale life beyond the realm of textbooks and research papers. She turned to waitressing to decompress from her stresses.

Her parents were both nurses. They were two kindred spirits, graduates of the renowned University of North Carolina at Chapel Hill's nursing school. Together, they chose a path illuminated by public service, adventure, and healing. United by their love for each other and their dedication to the underserved, they offered their expertise to those in need. They became wandering healers within the Peace Corps.

Camila's parents crisscrossed Central and South America for many years, offering care and kindness. From Guatemala's vibrant markets to Honduras's mist-covered mountains, their hands brought hope, their minds skill, and their hearts solace. Enjoying the vibrancy of each local culture and the resilience of each community, her parents worked long hours, day after day, year after year, without a desire to take a break. They dedicated their lives to their work, fully aware of the sacrifices their chosen path demanded. As dust stirred by the winds of change, they settled on their journey and welcomed their only child, Camila, into the world. Conceived in a poor Peruvian village and born amidst the volcanos of Guatemala, she symbolized their purpose and love.

One day, like many days, the setting sun painted the sky with hues of the coming evening while the day wound down, ordinary in its cadence. On this particular day, destiny wove a tale of human resilience and the profound impact of selfless service. The aftermath of a guerilla attack cast its pall and cried for aid. In a time of uncertainty, her parents emerged as beacons of hope. Within the makeshift tents of a Guatemalan field hospital, they wielded their medical expertise as instruments of healing, tirelessly tending to the wounded and infusing a surge of life into the surrounding darkness.

The wounded arrived, their faces etched in pain and terror, and her parents responded with unwavering resolve. They worked tirelessly, their skills honed by years of practice and dedication working far outside paradise's boundaries. Guided by their innate sense of humanitarianism, they set forth a sanctuary of care, their mission fueled by compassion rather than politics.

Marked by the beeps of battery-operated monitors and the hushed murmurs of the injured, the night wore on. Her parents held steadfast, their spirits unyielding, as they stitched wounds, administered medicine, and offered words of consolation to those clinging to the edge of life. The dawn of a new day revealed the many lives saved. The power of healing had once again bridged the chasm between life and death. The formerly pained faces bore traces of hope and gratitude. News of the valiant efforts of the Peace Corps and her parents' heroism echoed beyond the makeshift canvased hospital walls, ringing across the region. Strangers united by common humanity celebrated the tales of those who had stood firm.

Camila grew up with the pulse of the countries her parents served in years passed. But even with the tales of adventure and constant movement, she began to feel a twinge of isolation. Her parents, constantly embarking on a new episode in a new country, were her anchors but also the reason for her constant drifting. While she admired their dedication, she yearned for a place to call home, for friends who would remain, not a mere fleeting acquaintance. She often found herself wandering each hospital, seeking quiet corners and having to spend the nights gazing at stars in different positions, wondering if she would ever feel a sense of belonging. Her upbringing continued; her parents still served. They remained envoys of compassion, their legacy integrated into the lives they touched. Yet, as they journeyed from country to country and hospital to hospital, they began to hear the silent yearning within their daughter's heart.

When Camila reached high school age, her parents decided it was time to change the trajectory of their journey. Her parents returned to the United States to embrace their alma mater at Chapel Hill and brought Camila to America for the first time. With their experience and passion, her parents joined the faculty and began to shape the minds of future nurses, cultivating the spark of compassion in others. Within this newfound stability, Camila found the sense of belonging she had long sought and began to excel academically.

Chapel Hill, compared to their other homes, felt like its nickname, "the southern part of heaven." Relaxed, the family could consider thoughts beyond work. Previously, the notion of taking a vacation together had never come up in family conversations. The decision came after attending Sunday services at the Chapel of the Cross, an Episcopalian Church within walking distance from the University. In her sermon, the reverend began with a reference to the philosopher Onora O'Neill, "Our society is suffering from a crisis of trust." The fourteen-minute sermon was anchored around Doubting Thomas.

The reverend concluded her sermon by saying, "Thomas, a beacon of courage, stood amidst doubt, his voice resonating. His proclamation, rooted in a quest for truth, echoed a sentiment many of us dare to embrace – an audacious act to say, 'I won't believe until I see.' In a world where skepticism often dances with faith, we, too, embark on a parallel journey, risking vulnerability by uniting our voices to declare, 'We believe.' We entrust ourselves to the One who walked the path of liberation, the One who offered us the gift of light that guides our steps through the unknown. His presence infuses our lives with an essence of eternity, a reminder that the constraints of time do not bind our existence but are instead tinted by the hues of the divine. Gratitude cascades from our hearts, a river of appreciation for Thomas, whose skepticism unveiled the complexity of belief. Gratitude rises for Jesus, who repeatedly extends his presence to us, his love an unwavering thread that binds us together."

Camila's parents decided the message was an invitation to follow the steps of Saint Thomas. They decided to take a tour of Southern India. They began in Kerala, where the Apostle made landfall, then traveled down the coast to Kochi, calling in at the old synagogues. When they reached Kochi, they explored the waterside markets with their distinctive fishing nets and joined other local Christians at the Church of Saint Francis. They traveled through India's picturesque countryside to the temple city of Madurai to witness the evening ritual of the goddess Meenakshi. The Vaigai Express train took them to the old French colonial town of Pondicherry and then along the Coromandel Coast to the World Heritage site of Mahabalipuram. Their vacation culminated at Saint Thomas' tomb, where they ascended the mount to where he was martyred.

A child of curiosity and open-mindedness, Camila's spirit mirrored her parents'. When they returned home, they brought souvenirs of the trip and a legacy of togetherness and shared adventure. The vacation became a pilgrimage, a reaffirming chapter in their family story. Their experience yielded a celebration of exploration, showcasing the tenderness of faith and the deepening of bonds between souls.

Camila settled in at home and at school in Chapel Hill. She was always thin and scrawny, but she had physical strength beyond her size. During her adolescent and university years, she always appeared much younger than her actual age due to her lithe build and slim figure. In her early teens, she suffered from bouts of acne, but with guidance from her parents, her complexion soon cleared up. Her parents inspired her academic pursuits, and their dedication to their craft served as a lighthouse, illuminating the path toward a life of purpose. She aspired to walk in their footsteps, to tread the road of public service, carrying their torch forward. When the time came to choose her academic journey, her compass pointed her toward Georgetown University. The school tempted her passion for Environmental Biology, a topic she recognized could afford healing beyond the confines of a hospital.

The semesters unfurled like chapters in a book. Each page turned with zeal and dedication. Her aspirations grew, her dreams evolving into a mosaic of purpose and impact. The tales of her heroic parents provided the backdrop against which she would seek to forge her narrative. It would be etched with scholarly achievements and a commitment to the greater good. After the echoes of Georgetown subsided, her path led to Johns Hopkins to pursue her master's.

While at Georgetown, she tried establishing relationships beyond friendships and dabbled in dating. Her experience was nothing more than a long string of one-night stands. For months on end, her cycle was set on rinse and repeat. Among the dimly lit corners of a bar, she'd encounter a predictable pickup line. "Your mesmerizing eyes, they speak to me." Those words, meant to ignite a spark, led to a familiar ending – waking up beside someone whose presence held no lasting significance. On one occasion, she woke up alongside another woman. Each time, the dawn revealed an emptiness that mirrored the fleeting nature of these encounters.

Irrespective of her partner's physique, whether they boasted chiseled abs or carried extra weight around their middle, she had a consistent preference – occupying the superior position. Ascending to the top granted her a sense of dominion over the moment, a feeling she cherished. The confines of being beneath, owing to her petite stature, engendered a sensation of suffocation and unease she preferred to avoid. Aside from its psychological effects, this elevation offered her the coveted control over the rhythm of an intimate encounter. The dimensions of their bodies mattered little; her focus was on directing the ebb and flow of body movements. Her choice of music, reverberating from her phone, accompanied each escapade, though, to an observer, its playlist might have seemed more suited to an energetic aerobic workout routine. The initial melodies served as a warm-up to the more sensual subsequent motions. She followed each tempo, eschewing haste for a more deliberate and passionate unfolding of events. When the cadence of the music escalated, so did her intensity. Her routine required her partner to nestle her waist with their grasp while her palms settled upon their chest – this tactile connection an anchor, steering her thrusts with precision and intention.

She underwent a metamorphosis of sorts in the throes of the experience, her essence transformed by the cadence and crescendo. In her trance-like state, she became a virtuoso of Newtonian motion, eyes locked with her partner in a spellbinding communion. The intensity of her gaze, coupled with her ardent movement, often left her partner entranced, caught within the allure of her thrall, entrapped by the pleasure she concocted. However, as the musical journey shifted toward its denouement, her gaze's grip would slacken, a subtle detachment seeping in as the rhythm waned. This cooling-down phase was not only physical but also emotional – a sensation of feeling emotionless. It was as though, with each decrescendo, her ardor subsided, leaving her suspended in a contemplative reprieve. The playlist would end, and she separated from the moment and the victim beneath – a climatic rise and an anticlimactic fall.

However, her spirit remained steadfast. The sands of time washed away the remnants of these fleeting moments, leaving her untouched by their transient appeal. The passing faces and whispered promises were leaves carried away by the wind, leaving her rooted in her pursuit of knowledge. She recognized the search for connection was intricately intertwined with her dedication to her books and studies. Each encounter became a sign, a symbol guiding her towards a different path. Throughout her journey, she found solace in the pages of her textbooks and the sanctuary of her study sessions. Studying became more than a pursuit; it became her shield, refuge, and alibi. With each turning page, she embraced the companionship of knowledge, the steadfast bond by her side. Realms of academia filled her heart with who she was becoming, but the experiences growing up with her parents, she inherently knew to make time to find balance.

She departed the kitchen with another clean menu in her hand.

AND, MARTIN

"It's a pleasure to meet everyone and to be in such good company, albeit on this auspicious anniversary. I hope I wasn't interrupting anything." Martin looked around. "I thought the restaurant would be busier!"

"We believe the allure of room service has proven itself more favorable this morning," Otto said.

"Will Ms. Moytoy be by shortly?" Martin asked.

"Moments before you joined us, we discovered we'd meet her at the law office, which I thought was the original plan," Otto said.

"May I get you some coffee or juice? Here's our menu for this morning," Camila said.

"Thank you," Martin said. He thought the server looked very young – and distressingly thin. Her face appeared gaunt. But those eyes! The girl's green eyes spoke of things sexual, perhaps even forbidden.

"Are you getting hard," her eyes said.

"I'm sorry," Martin said. "What did you say?" He adjusted in his chair.

"May I get you some coffee or juice?"

"Chai, please."

"A pleasure. Would you like me to give you a minute to review the menu?"

"Certainly."

The waitress left to make Martin's tea. "Her eyes. How peculiar!" he said.

"I can't say I noticed," Otto said.

Linda suspected he was lying.

Two minutes later, the waitress returned with Martin's chai and placed it on the table to the right of his knife.

"Are you ready to order?"

"I'll just have a boiled egg," Martin said. Once again, her eyes captured his attention and he missed her question.

"I'm sorry," he said. "What did you just say?" He felt a twinge in his heart.

"Your boiled eggs. Would you like those hard?"

"Oh. Wet. I mean three minutes. Egg." Martin felt tongue-tied and tried to clear his throat. "Never mind, I'll just have a toasted cinnamon bagel with peanut butter. Thank you."

Quickly trying to shift the conversation, Martin enquired about everyone's journey and if they had a good trip. He also asked if anyone was affected by Geronimo. Linda went first and focused her story on changing a flat tire. While the all-male company didn't intimidate her, she wanted to clarify that testosterone and estrogen weren't the defining differences between all who sat at the breakfast table.

Martin jumped in when she finished, "Interestingly enough, I found myself in a similar situation yesterday. I happened upon an elderly couple looking desperate for help with a flat tire. They were pulled over on the shoulder of the interstate and waved for anyone to stop and help. It's so important to help one another. While my ticker doesn't have the prowess of my youth, it remains eager to assist. Actually, I'm on a list for a new one. So, if I'm lucky, perhaps I can regain some of that lost prowess. Anyway, I promptly summoned one of my capable aides to handle the tire change. My late arrival for breakfast also resulted from a telephone call this morning with this couple. I called to ensure their journey home was safe. What I thought would be a brief check-in evolved into a captivating conversation of well over an hour. They felt compelled to provide me with details of their life story, so I lent a patient ear – personal connection and all. I believe everyone should be made to feel significant. Man or woman. Extending a listening ear is never a burden. Indeed, fostering an environment where people genuinely believe their presence matters is a philosophy, I hold close to heart."

"How strange," Eli said. "I journeyed by car from Jersey. I tend to avoid flying from Newark when I can, especially on shorter trips. I must have encountered a half-dozen or more cars pulled over on the Jersey Turnpike at different points. Strangely enough, my eye failed to locate any telltale wreckage strewn across the highway to cause such an epidemic. I'm embarrassed to say that I didn't lend a hand to loosen the first lug nut. From what I could tell, the motley congregation of motorists all seemed capable of managing their predicaments. And certainly, far more capable than I. Given the bustling backdrop of the turnpike, I chose to stay my course rather than inadvertently sow any seeds for any further accidents."

"Your bagel, sir," the waitress said.

"Thank you," Martin said. Despite his reluctance, he made eye contact.

The stare was returned, and she said, "You're most welcome, sir."

Otto decided to pick up the mantle. He explained how Geronimo, with its metaphorical battle cry of "Geronimo," caused the FAA to shut down multiple major airport hubs, resulting in his scheduled flight from Nashville International Airport to Ronald Reagan Washington National Airport being canceled. "Without my asking, my driver volunteered to drive all the way here," he said. "We had some smooth sailing and a few rough patches. But with a sunny disposition, you can always find the good in the bad. Some sort of screwdriver fell off a passing vehicle and ruptured our tire. Elrod's remarkably capable and had the tire changed in no time. Elrod's my driver. Hopefully, he can get a new car this morning."

Otto didn't try to clarify or put into context his last statement. He was never one to seek pity or sympathy.

"I've never been married," Martin said. "I've been a bachelor all my life."

After seeing the waitress with her green eyes, those green eyes, he was moved to tell his story.

"Many years ago, I was engaged to be married. In the end, we weren't wed. It was not my decision to call things off, not hers. Allah, be praised. I don't think he could change things for us. I met her at our mosque in Harlem. She came to America on an education visa to study at Columbia. She had a brilliant mind. Her doctorate was to be in public health. She was a Muslim, of course. Her parents had supported her education, and she had done exceptionally well. She earned a master's degree in Hospital Administration from the Indian Institute of Public Health. She attained her bachelor's at the Indian Institute of Science in Environmental Science."

"Where did she grow up," Linda asked.

"I don't know too much about her family. Her parents were both nurses. Hardworking people, they were part of the Nomadic Nurses of Mercy. They traveled throughout India, working mainly in the areas of the disadvantaged. I believe Kalima – my fiancée's name – it means 'the word' – funny, for me, she always represented the first and last word in love. Anyway, Kalima told me she was born in a city along the southwest coast of India."

"By any chance, was that Kochi?" Otto asked.

"You're familiar with the city? I've never visited."

"It's known for having a large Christian-based community. It's been present there since the time of the Apostles," Otto said.

THE FLAT TIRE

Seeing Martin was becoming emotionally moved, a sympathetic Linda asked, "Are you okay?"

"Yes, yes. I'm fine. Now, where was I? Ah, yes. Kalima. Long years have since passed. Back then, my life had been adorned with the promise of a marital union. Ultimately, the promise was never fulfilled. The threads of matrimony eluded my grasp. Our grasp. This decree was not mine to render, nor was it hers to pronounce. Even Allah's hand hesitated to alter our course in life's fate."

Martin paused, looking into the empty dining room, but focused on nothing. Memories seeped into his consciousness. "The first thing I noticed about my fiancée when we met was her eyes. From the moment I saw them, I was imprisoned by their hold. I found them simply hypnotic. I'd say our waitress has her eyes if I didn't know any better. If my faith didn't lead me to believe otherwise, I'd say my Kalima had been reincarnated. But as a rational man, I know that can't be the case."

"What stopped the wedding?" Eli asked.

"Today's the anniversary of her passing. She was one of the many innocents caught up in the events."

"I'm sorry," Eli said.

"Thank you."

"May I offer anyone a refill on their drink," the waitress asked.

"Not for me," Otto said. "Thank you."

"I'm fine," Eli said.

"No, thank you," Linda said.

Martin shook his head and turned to look into Camila's eyes once more. Again, he felt a tug in his heart.

"I don't see a name tag. May I ask your name," Eli said.

"Camila."

All eyes looked at Martin. Martin closed his.

"Thank you, Camila," Eli said.

Camila walked away from the table and headed towards another guest.

"It's extraordinary how similar their names are," Linda said. "As an agnostic, even I'm taken a little aback."

Linda reached out her hand to place it on Martin's.

"That's terrible. It must be quite a shock for her memory to return to you this way?"

Martin could only muster a contemplative smile as the sunrays filtered through the window, casting a gentle glow over his face. Linda leaned forward.

Her words flowed like fragile petals drifting on the breeze. "Martin, during my journey, one thing I've observed in people is the profound desire to identify the correlations that shape our individual voyages. There's a longing desire to find threads linking causation with effect. I see many people who want to uncover these threads. Whether consciously or unconsciously, they seek help to validate their faith. Our waitress is not going to be the sign of correlation, meaning, or justification even though she may have ignited a moment of pain."

Martin's gaze, worn by the abundant memories of lost love, looked at his chai. "I've often pondered," he said. His voice was tinged with a mix of hope and uncertainty, "My faith acknowledges that some mysteries are beyond human understanding. People of faith know their perceptions are limited. Not every cause-and-effect relationship may be evident or ever present itself to us in our lifetime. My faith fosters a sense of humility and openness to the unknown."

"Easier said than done."

"Why a love as pure as ours was destined for such a tragic end, I'll never find out. But I can't set aside the pain of her passing. It has remained a chasm in my life – as raw as it is deep."

"In the theory of relativity, Einstein described the observer's perspective," Otto said. "Each observer has a unique frame of reference. The notion of theism will also yield different vantage points for you and your divine belief. Life is complicated!"

"I'd say that getting a rocket to Mars is *complicated*. Life, I describe it as *complex*," Eli said.

"Splitting hairs?" Otto asked.

"Perhaps, a little semantic, but I think Eli has a point." Martin reached out his hand and held it above one of Linda's uneaten croissants. "May I?" he asked.

"By all means," she replied.

Martin steered his erstwhile bagel plate to the side. He held the croissant. In front of his eyes and marveled at its crusty geometry. With one hand on each horn, he slowly destroyed the flaky perfection by increasing thumb pressure on either side. The croissant yielded. Crumbling cascades of fine bits fell to the table like so many shooting stars. What had once been a croissant was now an abstract collection flakes arranged in a delicate, though asymmetrical pyramid.

"There," he said. "This pile represents the second law of thermodynamics, the one dealing with entropy."

"That's a little out of my league," Otto said. "I tend to be a man of faith, not science."

"I am a lover of baked goods," Eli said. "What you just did is a crime against Nature." Everyone chuckled.

"God and science can coexist, Otto," Martin said. "Science doesn't rule out the existence of a creator. After all, there isn't a physicist or a mathematician who can tell you whether the Universe had a beginning. And, the Universe is separate from heaven."

"These people, these scientists, they talk about a big bang."

"That's fine. But scientists have no idea what existed before that point. Let's do this. What color is your napkin?"

"White," Otto said.

"Hold it up to Eli's face. I'm sure he won't mind if he gets a bit of egg on his face! Is Eli not white? Yet, the two whites are nothing alike. They both can't be white, can they? I think we can agree that our use of language allows room for ambiguity. So, while most of us agree Creation took six days…" he bobbed his head in acknowledgment of Linda's skepticism… "certainly a number of things occurred before there was day and there was night. Our language has plenty of wiggle room to accommodate a big bang and God."

"I get your point on language," Linda said. "I might say I'm running out to the grocery store to buy some milk and

THE FLAT TIRE

eggs and then return with two grocery bags full of other items. I'll still say, 'I got the milk and eggs,' and I may never declare the other items. Surely, in the best of circumstances, Genesis is allegorical. Even eating the fruit is nothing more than an allegorical story of evolution. Have you ever wondered why people say it's an apple Eve ate? The Bible doesn't tell us which fruit. You'll know this, Otto. The Latin word in the Vulgate for evil is *malum*. It's the same word the Romans used for 'apple.' It's a classic translation issue associated with language."

"If you're going to introduce allegory, we can view the Hebrew, *vayehi-erev vayehi-voker*," Eli said. "'And there was evening, and there was morning,' as nothing more than a declarative day of celebration for everything accomplished, even if it took billions of years to get done. If you will, it was the ticker tape parade lasting a day!"

"Anyway, let me get back to my point. Eli, would you please pass me the sugar bowl?"

Although Eli knew Martin could have leaned over to grab it, he handed over the bowl. In the space between the crumpled croissant and his teacup, Martin further shocked everyone by emptying the sugar onto the table.

"Now, if I pinch a little sugar from the pile and then let it fall again. You'll see the shape of the pile of sugar remains unchanged. Here, I'll do it again. See? The sugar has high entropy. The croissant was low entropy. While these concepts may be a little difficult, they aren't complex because the physics behind all of this is understood although certainly better by other people. But, since everything works in a consistent and reliable manner, scientists can work the problem. Ergo, the situation is *complicated*. On the other hand, people aren't consistent and reliable when it comes to behaviors. People can act out on something for no apparent reason. They don't abide by the laws of the Universe. They abide by free will, resulting in highly *complex* situations."

"The enigma of human behavior captivates each of us," Otto said. "It casts an irresistible spell to which we are drawn."

"I agree with Otto," Martin said. "Recently, I had some business in Brooklyn. I was walking through Prospect Park on my way to Flatbush. It was a nice sunny day, not too hot, but I thought I'd take a short break to relax, sit on a bench, and people-watch for a while. I observed this woman who looked to be in her mid-twenties. There was no telltale sign of eccentricity about her. Her hair was tidy, her clothes were clean looking, nothing unusual. Yet, there she was, kneeling by the path, tending to an injured pigeon. I thought, 'This is not average behavior for a New Yorker!' Her act appeared to unfold entirely in the moment, driven by a surge of empathy and compassion. For me, it's difficult to fathom whether her behavior was rooted in logic and reason. On the other hand, does every action require such firm grounding? After all, actions influenced by raw emotion or spontaneous impulse don't always warrant a negative connotation. Isn't the capacity to exhibit a spectrum of behaviors, making us a complex species, inherently a strength?"

"Aren't they full of diseases?" Linda asked. "The pigeons."

"Yes, but the pathogens they carry aren't generally fatal," Martin said.

"If everyone acted solely on rationality and commonsense, where every action was calculated toward a predefined goal, such a world would lack vibrancy and depth. Impulsiveness and spontaneity are assets," Otto said.

"No doubt we all come across people in our mosques, churches, synagogues, and classrooms who present themselves with warmth and kindness only to reveal ulterior motives later that leave us bewildered."

"Indeed," Otto said.

"Cardinal, you seek power and control. Rabbi, I've noticed you are searching for redemption and a little something extra to ease your Jewish guilt. And, my dear doctor, you seek nothing more than a seat at the table," Martin said.

Everyone looked at Martin with eyes squinted and mouths agape. Since no one spoke, the Imam continued. "People can wear a mask, a façade, to gain trust and access to resources while concealing their true intentions. This is a face of complexity. Many individuals might genuinely care for others, but undercurrents of self-interest can unduly influence their actions. People can develop a sense of wariness, knowing that appearances can be deceiving. Many behaviors are driven by desire. Self-interest adds layers of unpredictability; we're all beings of agency, capable of shaping destinies through intentions and choices. While some actions might appear erratic or contradictory, they'll often arise from an intricate interplay of factors outside our purview. Our parents, upbringing, cultural context, personal aspirations, and the complexities of emotions will influence behaviors. This all makes dealing with life very complex," Martin said. "Impulsively, people can be driven by momentary desires, only later overtaken by regret or conflicting emotions."

"I agree with what you are saying," Otto said. "Many people will make a spontaneous decision counterintuitive to what they seek. It certainly leaves one befuddled. But this is why we must be careful how we shepherd our flocks."

Jabari cleared his throat from behind Otto. "I apologize for the intrusion," he said.

Everyone stopped talking.

"I've just been informed your escort to Ms. Moytoy's office has arrived and is waiting in the hotel lobby."

"My goodness, the time has flown," Otto said.

"Can we get the check," Eli asked.

"Everything has been taken care of for you," Jabari said. "How was everything this morning?"

"Very good. And, please forgive the mess!" Martin said. He pointed to the crumpled croissant and pile of sugar. "We were discussing the Big Bang!"

"That's quite all right. We've certainly cleaned up worse."

"Can you thank our waitress for us," Linda asked.

"Certainly, I hope you have a wonderful day."

"Let the person in the lobby know we'll be one more minute," Linda said. "I want to get something from my room before we head over."

"*One minute* – another one of those language ambiguities," Otto said with a wink.

Martin looked over toward the dining room's centerpiece, the grand, meticulously crafted sideboard with its display of tall vases holding exotic flowers of vibrant color, and saw Camila arranging some silverware. She looked over in his direction, and their eyes met. Martin felt another twinge.

PART III

SEQUOIA

Sequoia Moytoy is proud of her family heritage. She is a member of the *Ani-Yun-Wiya*, the Principal People. Anybody who engages with Moytoy, Bissouma, Porro, Son, and Postecoglou learns firsthand about the importance of her indigenous background – a heritage preceding the Nina, the Pinta, and the Santa Maria. Sequoia is part of the Cherokee Nation.

Sequoia knew her life would have a purpose beyond the boundaries of the poverty choking her people's reservation. With unwavering resolve, she embarked on a journey to Harvard Law School on a full scholarship. Her life's transition was both exhilarating and daunting. She swam in a sea of aspiring legal minds, each with unique aspirations and stories. But Sequoia carried with her the wisdom of her ancestors, the resilience of her people, and a fierce determination to succeed and excel.

Her days at Harvard Law School were a whirlwind of

rigorous studies, passionate debates, and endless hours of research. With each case and lecture, Sequoia felt more attuned to the intricacies of the law. She was not just learning about precedents, she was also immersing herself in the legacy of the law and its potential for change.

Enthusiastically engaged, Sequoia wholeheartedly plunged into Harvard's vibrant Native American Program. Within its nurturing embrace, she found herself enriched by the wisdom of trailblazing minds – pioneers who harnessed their brilliance to illuminate the path for excellence in academia, literature, arts, and the discipline of indigenous studies.

On one such occasion, a lecture titled "The Trouble with Tragedy," carried with it a soul-resonating message. The speaker, a luminary hailing from the Leech Lake Band of Ojibwe, held a torch of transformation, igniting the possibilities of self-belief and resilience. His voice helped cultivate intricate thought patterns to, "Redeclare your own personal independence." Sequoia was drawn into a place where limitations were redefined, challenges became stepping stones, and adversity catalyzed growth. Sequoia's heart found resonance with the stories of those who defied the odds, carried the ancestral wisdom within their spirits, and unveiled the limitless indigenous potential. The lecture ignited a spark within her – an illuminating spark. It reinforced her commitment to her people and lit a flame of self-belief.

Guided by the lecture's echoes, Sequoia embarked on a journey of transformation – a trek marked by her academic pursuits and a fanatical determination to uplift her community, amplify indigenous voices, and reshape narratives of possibility. With each step, she bore the torch of self-belief, recognizing resilience and brilliance were interwoven, ever-present, and unbreakable in her heritage.

Sequoia stood as a testament to the speaker's words – a living embodiment of the power of self-belief, the magic of transformation, and the boundless potential within the hearts of indigenous individuals. She ventured forth carrying the lecture's lessons like intellectual treasure.

Graduation approached; Sequoia's dreams crystallized. She envisioned building a world-class law firm, offering a broad range of services but specializing in constitutional law and advocating for the rights of indigenous communities, underserved populations, and those whose voices often went unheard. Her aspiration was to create a firm that could shine in the courtroom. Moreover, she pictured a powerhouse so formidable adversaries would tremble at the mere mention of her firm's name, resulting in concessions to the demands of her clients and forgoing litigation. Above all, her firm would serve as a beacon of empowerment for those it represented.

With her degree in hand, Sequoia returned to the Cherokee Nation, her heart brimming with a sense of commitment. She knew this was just beginning. Drawing from the strength of her ancestors and the knowledge she had gained, she embarked on the arduous task of starting her law firm and attracting deep-pocketed clients.

She earned her first law license from the Cherokee Bar

Association. At her swearing-in ceremony, her parents and siblings heard her proudly declare in clear, annunciated words, "I do solemnly swear that I will, to the best of my knowledge and ability, support and defend all causes that may be entrusted to my care, and that in so doing, I will be true to the court and to the constitution and laws of the Cherokee Nation and subject myself to the contempt powers of the Cherokee Nation Courts. So, help me, God." She signed an oath declaring the same, handed it over to the Court Clerk of the Cherokee Nation Supreme Court, and subsequently paid her fifty-dollar annual Bar dues fee in cash.

Soon after, she took and passed the Oklahoma Bar. With her future plotted out, she took the Washington, D.C. Bar and was waived into Maryland and Virginia. After she had three years of practice under her belt, she applied for admission to the Supreme Court. She was also admitted to the Court of Appeals for the Federal Circuit.

In her early years of practicing law, she fought tirelessly to pass legislation, including a resolution authorizing the Cherokee Nation to sell real estate to the Housing Authority of the Cherokee Nation, a resolution to support investment in Cherokee Nation Emergency Medical Services funded under the Respond, Recover, and Rebuild Plan, and a resolution objecting to the United States Environmental Protection Agency grant of environmental regulatory jurisdiction to the State of Oklahoma. She was winning allies and making herself known.

Building a blue-ribbon law firm is not without its

challenges and requires more than legal acumen. Looking for savviness, dedication, and an unwavering commitment, she sought partners who could bring with them an esteemed list of paying clients. Sequoia worked tirelessly, combining her growing legal expertise with a deep understanding of indigenous communities' unique needs and challenges.

Years passed, and her law firm flourished – not beyond her wildest dreams, for this was precisely her vision. Its reputation as a champion of constitutional rights spread far and wide, attracting a diverse clientele from across the nation. The firm opened offices overseas with the same mission: to help indigenous communities and to represent the underserved. Success was not measured in financial gains, though she never underestimated money's power. Success was measured by the lives she impacted, the communities she empowered, and the legacy she was building for future indigenous generations.

She took on four principal partners, each a renowned legal scholar and each with the potential for a seat on the U.S. Supreme Court. Yves Bissouma was the first to join Sequoia. He could trace his family lineage to the Ivory Coast and show how his family suffered in the first wave of injustices brought into Jamestown. Pedro Porro heralded from Las Cruces in Mexico. He claimed to have a bloodline tracing back to the Mayans. Heung-min Son was an ex-pat from South Korea. Ange Postecoglou was born in Australia of Greek descent but came to America before he started grade school. Sequoia's global team of dedicated attorneys, paralegals, and support staff shared her passion for justice and commitment to upholding constitutional rights. Together, they navigated complex legal battles, challenged systemic injustices, and secured landmark victories.

Beyond the courtroom, she actively engaged with the Cherokee Nation and other indigenous communities, conducting workshops, providing legal education, and fostering a sense of unity. She understood the fight for justice required the support of a community believing in the power of change. Sequoia's name became synonymous with courage, resilience, and unwavering dedication. Her journey from the Cherokee Nation to Harvard Law School and back had come full circle and she gave back to the communities that shaped her. She represented a living testament to the possibilities of achievement when heritage and passion converge with determination.

Despite the demands of her lengthy work hours, the Cherokee Nation remained a steadfast presence in her heart and thoughts. The sobering realization her people did not own their reservation land struck a deep, painful chord. Instead, the lands were held in trust by the United States – a bitter truth that cut deep.

Growing up on the reservation, she was immersed in the culture and traditions of the Cherokee Nation. The donated land beneath her feet bore the footprints of generations past, and the winds whispered generational tales. Her parents were pillars of strength in her life. Their parenting style was rooted in love, discipline, and a deep respect for the tribe's values. They instilled in her and her siblings the

THE FLAT TIRE

importance of community, family, and a strong connection to the land. Every evening, as the sun painted the sky, her father would gather the family to share stories of their ancestors, passing down the wisdom from generations in an unbroken chain.

Sequoia was the eldest of four siblings, and as such, she often found herself taking on a nurturing role. She looked after her younger brothers, teaching them the art of storytelling and sharing the joy of exploring the forests surrounding their home. Their days were filled with laughter, adventure, and a deep sense of kinship.

Playtime for her was a blend of traditional Cherokee games and imaginative play. With her friends, she chased after rolling hoops, competed in stickball matches, and invented stories inspired by the legends of their people. Their laughter would echo through the valleys as they reveled in the simple joys of childhood.

She attended a small, single-room schoolhouse. The close-knit community institution honored Cherokee culture. She learned the basics of reading, writing, and arithmetic as well as the Cherokee language, history, and arts. The community elders often visited the school to impart their wisdom and teachings.

Food was an integral part of her upbringing. Her family relied on traditional Cherokee crops, cultivating beans, corn, and squash, known as the "Three Sisters." These staples were foundational ingredients for their meals, nourishing their bodies and strengthening their connection to the land. She cherished the gatherings around the fire, where her family would savor dishes like bean soup, cornbread, and wild game.

Yet, despite the beauty of their culture and traditions, she was not blind to the challenges surrounding her. Poverty cast a shadow over the reservation, affecting many families, including her own. She witnessed her parents working tirelessly to provide for the family, and even then, ends sometimes barely met. It was a reality she accepted with a mixture of resilience and determination. Still, the community came together with a spirit of solidarity. Her family shared what they had, extending a helping hand to their neighbors in times of need. She saw the strength emanating from unity, the way the Cherokee people upheld one another through difficult times.

She grew older and began to understand the importance of education in breaking the cycle of poverty. She continued to work hard in school, embracing her Cherokee heritage while looking forward to a future where she could make a difference. She dreamt of becoming a lawyer, a voice for her community, advocating for justice, equality, and above all, equity.

Her life unfolded against the backdrop of the Cherokee Nation – a journey marked by love, family, cultural pride, and an unyielding determination to rise above adversity. Her experiences on the reservation shaped her into a strong, compassionate young woman, ready to embrace the challenges and opportunities ahead. As the sun set over the rolling hills, casting a warm glow on the land into which her roots sank, she stood poised to create her own path while carrying the legacy of her people in her heart.

In the picturesque landscapes of northwest Georgia, Sequoia's path intersected with her future husband's – a fellow member of the Cherokee Nation. Their serendipitous encounter unfolded during one of her hiking expeditions. She had traveled to behold the historic grounds of the former Cherokee capital, New Echota. This hallowed site, as some cruel joke, had been lovingly transformed into a preserved state park. Amid the rolling beauty of the land, at the confluence of the Coosawattee and Conasauga rivers, Walks the Sky found solace in the art of trout fishing. His soul resonated with the gentle cadence of the rivers, the congruent ripples of water carrying echoes of generations past – a shared passion for nature served as the bridge connecting their paths on the joyful day of their meeting.

As luck would have it, neither Sequoia nor Walks the Sky were accompanied by companions. It was as if destiny had conspired to shape their future lives. With a heart open to possibility, Sequoia approached him, her footsteps flowing with the cadence of the rivers nearby. A conversation sparked, a connection, subtle yet profound. Curiosity danced in the air while Sequoia posed a question, her voice carried by the whispering wind. She inquired about his choice to fish in contaminated waters. His response, offered with a pearl of quiet wisdom, revealed a richer truth: "It's not about the fishing; it's about the connection with the past." In those words, the essence of their shared heritage reverberated.

The once-pristine lands, formerly tended with care by the Cherokee, had fallen victim to modernization's encroachment. The textile industry, once a promise of progress, had left its mark on the waters flowing through the region. Polyfluoroalkyls, known ominously as "forever chemicals" because they defied degradation, had seeped into the streams. Their presence was a harsh reminder of the fragile balance between progress and preservation, a reminder that Nature's scars were often borne by those who cherished Nature itself.

Throughout this poignant conversation alongside the gentle flow of the river and beneath the boundless celestial reflection, Sequoia and Walks the Sky unearthed a calling transcending any other relationship they had known. They recognized an allure kindling an iridescent glow within their souls. Their connection was not merely the fusion of shared histories. It was a cauldron for mutual dreams and aspirations. In the soft cadence of the wind, their hearts entwined and gave life to a precious gift – a healthy baby boy.

The rays of the sun embraced the land. Walks the Sky, his heart brimming with pride, pondered names to encapsulate the significance of this new life. "Laredo," he suggested. "It's a name evoking a top-of-the-line Grand Cherokee."

Sequoia was not amused. For years, she had remained incensed when a foreign car manufacturer coopted her name for commercial gain. Together, the young couple discovered the perfect name: Seattle, a name resonating with thoughtful meaning and denoting "a man of high status" in their native tongue. Moreover, it wasn't a label sported by a passenger vehicle.

In the Cherokee Nation, where the past and present danced in congruence, and the wind carried ancient secrets, Seattle's name represented a beacon of hope and a testament to the enduring power of their love – one they hoped would transcend time, enrich their heritage, and kindle fire to illuminate the path ahead.

A master of financial endeavors, Walks the Sky operated his own hedge fund. He secured prosperity and facilitated success for indigenous entrepreneurs who sought to grow their ventures by providing capital and mentorship. His purpose was as vast as the heavens themselves and helped to foster growth and empowerment for all tribes. When in diverse company, he humbly requested to be addressed as "Bob," an embodiment of his straightforward, down-to-earth nature. No frills, no formalities – "Just call me Bob."

His office was not beholden to the confines of four walls. Armed with a laptop and a wireless internet connection, he wielded his financial prowess from wherever the winds of opportunity led him. He could learn more about his clients and investors by seeing their eyes than during a faceless, "I'm not camera ready" Zoom call. Had he occupied an office, it would have been akin to caging a wild spirit.

Walks the Sky was not a solitary star. He was a devoted husband, a partner who cherished the moments shared with Sequoia and Seattle. His role as a father transcended geography, for even in the whirlwind of business travel, he dedicated time to nurturing the familial bond.

Sequoia was a force of her own. Whenever she traveled for work, she never had to go alone. Untethered to a desk, Walks the Sky could travel with her and Seattle. Together, they worked and played, side by side, a testament to their unwavering unity. Their son was the heartbeat of their existence. His young world grew rich with attention, affection, and connection. In the middle of bustling schedules, his parents carved out spaces for family togetherness, ensuring his childhood did not lack laughter, play, and shared moments. They treated him as their constant, their guiding star.

Their story portrayed a vivid portrait of balance, an intricate harmony of professional dreams and profound private moments. Mingled within the hustle and bustle of the day-to-day, the family reveled in the simple yet extraordinary joy of a life well-lived. They shared a life shimmering with accomplishment, resonated with love, and soared like eagles in flight.

Their spiritual beliefs pranced – fireflies in the night. The Cherokees hold a deep reverence for the natural world, where every rock, tree, and creature is infused with a spirit – a life force interconnected with all living things. They believe the Creator gave life – sacred life – to the world. Consequently, the family's rituals, prayers, and daily actions reflected this profound respect for Nature. Maintaining harmony between the physical and spiritual realms was essential for Sequoia, Walks the Sky, and Seattle's well-being. Their beliefs guided their interactions with the land, animals, tribal members, and fellow humans.

The Cherokee practice a form of animism, where they communicate with the spirits of Nature through ceremonies and rituals. Each year, the family traveled to Oklahoma to be with the Cherokee Nation and participate in the Green Corn Ceremony. Held during the first new moon of summer, the ceremony represented a cornerstone of their spiritual calendar. This was a time of renewal, purification, and gratitude. It also marked the beginning of the agricultural cycle and helped to emphasize unity within the tribe.

Since the Cherokee also believe in the power of dreams and visions, Sequoia and Walks the Sky talked with the Dreamers, spiritual leaders who interpreted dreams as messages from the spirit world. These communications helped guide the family and offered insights into essential decisions and healing.

Sequoia would take Seattle into the sweat lodge, a small, dome-shaped structure symbolizing the womb of Mother Earth. She would help him cleanse himself in the sacred space through steam, prayer, and singing. She told her son stories that cherished tradition and helped bridge the generational gap. Outside, elders would gather the young around the fire, recounting myths, legends, and ancestral tales. These stories entertained and established a way to impart moral lessons, cultural values, and an understanding of the world's mysteries.

MILLER

THE CENTER OF THE HOTEL LOBBY HAD TWO SEATING AREAS for guests. One was framed by twin, handmade Chesterfield-inspired sofas and a pair of wingback chairs, all encased in matching oxblood leather and adorned with ample tufts and studs. Each sofa was large enough to seat four large adults in contentment. The seats were arranged around a six-foot square sycamore wood coffee table with steel tube legs in a U-shape. The two wingbacks shared a taller side table placed between them. Toward the entrance to the U, three stacks of newspapers were lined up on the edge of the coffee table. The smell of fresh ink wafted across the area like an unwelcome guest.

Geronimo was grabbing the day's headlines. *The Washington Post* blazoned in a bold font, "Geronimo's Revenge." The hurricane's winds and rain had caused havoc in the south. Thousands of people were stranded or displaced as the rain flooded towns and roadways, and the rivers rose high above their banks. One byline complained about how urban planners have been getting away with murder for far too long: "Stop covering up your impermeable land use mistakes under the pretense of severe weather." Governors from several states declared a state of emergency. Teams of administrators and doers from the Federal Emergency Management Administration and the Red Cross arrived to provide immediate relief. The outer bands of Geronimo were due into the D.C. area later in the day, with the current sunshine likely to be the last for the next forty-eight to seventy-two hours.

Camila Soto was three weeks into an eight-week internship at the prestigious Moytoy, Bissouma, Porro, Son, and Postecoglou law firm. She was born and raised in Puerto Rico and was in her final year at the David A. Clarke School of Law at the University of the District of Columbia. Her family's connection to the institution ran deep, and she had been accepted as a legacy admission. She'd grown up listening to her father and grandfather's vivid accounts of their years at the university. One of the classrooms even bore her grandfather's name.

When she first met the admissions officer, she was greeted with a warm smile and a message, "Legacy admissions carry with them a rich history. It's not just about familial ties but the continuation of a tradition, a commitment to upholding the values for which this law school stands. Remember, Camila, your character, dedication, and desire to contribute must come from you. Those things can't be inherited."

Upon leaving the admissions office, she wandered through the campus, each step echoing the footfalls of generations past. She stood before a mural inscribed with a poem, "This I Believe." She was scheduled to graduate next spring and was proud to have attained her internship based solely on her own merits and not her family's. The opening stanza from the poem flooded her mind, "I believe the day will come when rich and poor will stand equal before the law. And I believe the day will come when Black and White, Hispanic, Asian, and Native American, young and old, man and woman, will stand equal before the law."

She had been tasked with escorting her party to the law office across the street. But this was no ordinary party – a cardinal, a rabbi, an imam, and a doctor. It was an intimidating crew for the intelligent but bubbly young upstart, but she felt equal to the challenge. She would be responsible for collecting and delivering her party safely and in one piece to the "Teehee" conference room.

Camila stood and waited beside the arm of one of the large Chesterfields. One eye was on the elevator bank, the other on the rotating door separating the lobby from the street. A parade of black Suburban SUVs streamed by the lobby windows, one after the other – so many she quickly lost count.

Linda was the first to arrive in the lobby. She noticed a woman holding an iPad waist-high with the law firm's name in red letters on a white background.

"Good morning, I'm Doctor Herzog. And you are?"

"Camila. How are you? Are you having an enjoyable

THE FLAT TIRE

stay? You're the first to arrive. We have to wait for three others."

"You're very effervescent! I was just with the others, and they should all be down shortly. Everyone had to stop by their rooms after breakfast. Camila! Our waitress, that was her name too."

"I've been told the breakfasts are huge here. They give you so much food."

"I just had half a croissant."

"Where are you from?"

The small pleasantries continued. Camila was happy she could speak clearly enough to carry on a conversation.

"What's going on outside?" Linda asked.

Camila looked over her shoulder to see what was happening. Several police officers on motorcycles rode by the hotel with lights flashing but no sirens.

"What's going on outside?" Martin asked.

"Oh, hello, Martin. I didn't see you creep up! This is our greeter, Camila. I know, right? We were just wondering the same thing about all those police."

"I saw some black vehicles drive by a few minutes ago. I assumed they were Secret Service transporting some dignitary or something. There's always so much going on here. I don't know if this is associated with that," Camila said. "Hello, I'm Camila." She shook Martin's hand. "I'm here to take you over and get you all checked in as soon as the others arrive."

At this point, the leading edge of the protestors appeared, walking past the hotel with their signs. The hotel doors and windows provided a high degree of soundproofing, so it was difficult to determine if they walked in silence or if their chants simply couldn't be heard.

Unbeknownst to the collecting group, the White House was to receive a guest who many claimed was formally part of a breakaway faction of White Supremacists. The woman had staunchly denied such involvement. With the fine line she walked during her speeches, it was difficult to tell where the truth lay. But in an era of real-time revisionist history, facts were dependent on the observer. Those who won the right to influence could form the facts and shape the truth as they deemed appropriate. The woman had been scheduled to meet in the afternoon, and the group of protesters were going to rally at that time. However, with the impending arrival of Geronimo, the hosting calendars had been cleared for the remainder of the week. Not wanting to waste a trip, the protesters moved their march to midmorning. After all, they were already in town, and there was no point in getting unnecessarily wet.

"Why let the rain ruin a perfectly good outfit, sweetie," would be heard from one of the protesters later in the day on the evening news.

These same gaggle had also marched during Pride Month. Some participated in events in other countries, such as Armenia, Romania, and The Netherlands. Pride was a season designed to celebrate the lives and experiences of LGBTQ+ communities and to protest against attacks on hard-won civil rights gains. Today, they were out in force again.

THE FLAT TIRE

While America is United in name, life in America remains divided. The protesters, aware of the contentious political climate, knew that any action had to be peaceful. Congress had voices determined to use their positions as a soapbox to oppose burlesque bars and drag shows, prohibit gender-affirming care, and restrict teachers' speech about sexuality and gender in the classroom.

"You can't keep our communities down. No one can. We have the same basic human rights as every other person," had been a podcast sentiment making the rounds for quite some time.

Despite the attempt to protest peacefully, violence often ensued. Killings were not uncommon.

During this year's Pride Month, New York City's *Village Voice* reported on the actions of protesters protesting one another, "What we're seeing right now is probably the worst that it's been since the early days." Other Pride marches, such as those hosted in San Francisco and Chicago, occurred without incident. Pride organizers create a wide-ranging set of activities, from readings and performances to parties and street festivals, and even go so far as to coordinate events across the world, from Sao Paulo to Tel Aviv and from Madrid to Toronto.

Some of the chants from the street were starting to emanate into the lobby. Shouts of "Reclaim Pride" could be heard.

Tomorrow's *Washington Post* would run a story with the quotation, "We're going to fight back against the very oppressive forces that are coming for us." The President would also say, "Transgender Americans deserve to be safe and supported in every community. Again, I am denouncing the hundreds of hateful and extreme state laws that target transgender families."

"What's going on out there?" Otto asked.

Camila turned to face Otto. She saw Eli standing next to him. "Hello, I'm Camila. I'll be taking you over to the office. And you are?" she asked, extending her hand toward Otto.

"Hello, and I'm Ezekiel," Eli said, shaking her hand. "It's a pleasure to meet you. We're meeting a lot of women named Camila this morning. That was also the name of our waitress."

"There's a protest moving past the hotel. We'll wait until they've walked by and then head over. I'll text Ms. Moytoy to let her know we'll walk over once the coast is clear. I want to keep you all safe," she said with an assertive smile.

Eli started to ask a question when, from outside, a mighty crash sounded followed by a series of hysterical screams. The strident sounds filled the lobby just before a body crashed through one of the windows.

Someone shouted, "Call nine-one-one – now!"

Barely half a minute before, the electrical heartbeat of a Tesla Plaid pulsed as it emerged from the depths of a parking garage onto F Street, where it intersected with the bustling energy of Eleventh Street. A leisurely drive carried it westward, a journey punctuated by the glow of a verdant traffic light at Twelfth Street, an implied nod from the Universe to proceed. As the car approached the intersection of Thirteenth Street, progress was

THE FLAT TIRE

momentarily halted, brought about by the emergence of a crimson light.

Behind the wheel, the driver reached for her phone and placed a call the world would remember. Simultaneously, a group of resolute individuals embarked on a mission. Feet met asphalt, setting forth a tide of purposeful strides as they ventured onto the crosswalk at Fourteenth Street. They stopped. Their intent was clear: to claim dominion over the intersection to prevent north-south passage.

The driver's foot pressed heavily against the accelerator when the light turned green. A battle cry leaped from her vocal cords and hung in the cabin's air, "Geronimo," with an extended "oh" that didn't end until the car stopped. With its accident prevention electronics disengaged, the eleven hundred brake horsepower machine sprung forward like a scalded cat. It reached its top speed of one hundred and sixty miles per hour in mere seconds. In eerie silence, the Tesla streaked along the asphalt surface. Even though it traveled five times slower than a nine-millimeter bullet, it was over six feet wide and three hundred thousand times heavier. Metal met flesh in a sickening cataclysm of cracking bones, spewing blood, and other-worldly shrieks. The human block of protesters transformed into a playground of chaos. Bodies flew through the air like spastic marionettes. The Tesla's path was ultimately halted by the unyielding high five with the cast iron safety pylons in front of the U.S. Treasury Building.

Pandemonium reigned supreme. Once the initial shock abated, bewilderment and fear took hold. In the aftermath, the car sat immobile, its serenity starkly contrasting to the chaos it had unleashed. The driver enveloped in a cocoon of safety measures, emerged from the vehicle shaken but unscathed. A modern-day Prometheus, the driver was saved by a crash helmet, airbags, a seat harness, and the fortitude of engineering that defined the car's safety cage. Once a sentinel of protection, the helmet was cast aside beside the rear flat tire.

With one step, the driver merged into the crowd, one figure among many, faceless and lost inside the milling throng. In the story of the moment – the collision, the chaos, the survival – the catalyzing agent blended into the erupting confusion.

"What the hell?" Eli recoiled from the torso thrown in the lobby. Screams rushed in through the shattered window.

"Stay with me," Linda said.

"They'll need our help," Otto said. He began a silent prayer. *Divine Creator, we are in a moment of profound turmoil and upheaval. I humbly come before you as a spectator to this unfolding disaster. My heart already aches as I bear witness to the pain and suffering that have befallen those around me. I beseech you, O Compassionate One, to extend your healing grace to all those affected by this active tragedy. May your boundless love envelop them, offer solace to the wounded, strength to the weary, and comfort to the grieving. May our collective human spirit rise above the darkness, uniting us in a shared commitment to support and uplift one another. In your infinite grace, I place my trust and my prayer in my Lord Jesus Christ. Amen.*

THE FLAT TIRE

Shocked by what he saw, Martin said, "In Your name, O Allah, I seek comfort and relief. May your mercy embrace me in this moment of despair, and may your blessings illuminate my path toward hope and healing. Amen." He looked at the others. "I agree with Otto. We've no time to lose. Come."

Outside, no one knew if the worst was over or if there was more to come. Some fled the area; others stayed. Voices shouted for medical attention; there were screams of agony. Linda remained in the lobby with Camila and attended to people staggering inside.

"Find out if they have bottles of water. See if housekeeping can bring clean towels," Linda said as she directed her toward a concierge manager. "Go."

While Camila left to find supplies, Linda waded into the melee within the lobby. Otto, Eli, and Martin chose to hurry outside. Each took stock of the catastrophe and, without a word, started walking in different directions, searching for anyone they could reasonably help. Martin saw a man lying over the curb between the sidewalk and the road.

"What hurts?" Martin asked.

"My back. I can't move my legs," the man said.

"An ambulance will be here any second," Martin said. "It's important for you to stay conscious if you can. What happened?"

"I didn't see anything. All of a sudden, I was flying through the air." He faked a grin. "I guess being Superman isn't everything I imagined as a kid. I landed on my back – I think it's broken."

"Are you a man of faith?"

"Buddhist."

Go figure! Martin thought. *It had to be one this morning's Breakfast Club didn't have covered.*

"What's your name, son,"

"Miller, sir," the man said. "But my parents baptized me, Kamila, with a 'K.' They're Southern Baptists. They wouldn't understand."

The comment did not register, but Martin was familiar with how people looked when going into shock and could see a pool of blood appearing around his head.

"Hold on, son. Stay with me."

"I hope my life has not been meaningless," Miller's voice was barely audible.

Martin knew CPR. He pulled open his shirt. Miller had a woman's body. Martin blinked several times to clear his head, then started compressions. Miller did not respond. The air was now filled with the wailing sound of sirens approaching from multiple directions. An ambulance materialized alongside Martin and Miller.

"Here, here," Martin shouted as a team of emergency medical technicians appeared.

A medic rushed over.

"I've attempted CPR, but he needs more. I fear it's not enough. Can you assist me in rising to my feet? I'm feeling a little giddy."

The paramedic, a paragon of compassion and training, met his eyes with a nod of acknowledgment and, with steady hands, helped Martin back to his feet.

THE FLAT TIRE

The paramedic pursed his lips. "Are you injured?"

"No, no. I'm fine. Please, this man needs your help. I've attempted CPR, but he may have a back injury, and as you can see, there's blood." Martin felt his heart twinge again. "I'll need to go inside and sit down," he said as much to himself as to the paramedic. Martin took one more look at the man and said, "May Miller and his bereaved family find comfort. Compassionate Buddha, please accept this sincerest prayer. Allah be praised."

Taking measured steps, he made his way back to the lobby. The intensity of the situation pounded on him in waves of grief. He made his way over to the Chesterfields and found a seat. Camila noticed him and immediately walked over and offered him a bottle of water.

"Can I get you something else?" she asked.

"I just need a moment. Thank you."

Linda was busy applying a tourniquet to a woman's arm.

"Let me help you," a voice said. It was the waitress from the morning's breakfast. "I've been around doctors and nurses most of my life. Please let me show you the correct way to tie a tourniquet."

Surprised, Linda pulled back and gave the waitress room.

"Like this. See. Avoid placing it over the joint; don't make it too loose or tight. I've watched my parents do this many times. They used to work in field hospitals for the Peace Corps. I will be getting my doctorate in Public Health at Johns Hopkins. I'm just taking a few months off."

I misjudged this book cover, Linda thought. "Much

appreciated." Pointing, she said, "There are others over there that could use your help."

In the unfolding hours, Otto, Eli, Linda, and Martin shared a collective spirit of compassion. Their actions became vital in consoling the injured, the dying, and those in grief. Prayers were offered, a whispered bridge connecting the earthly and the ethereal. Hearts were heavy for everyone involved. In each utterance, they provided a measure of comfort, a balm for visible and undetected wounds.

"I've texted Ms. Moytoy to let her know I'll bring everyone over once the police have given the all-clear."

"Thank you," Linda said.

"I dare say that our presence here this morning came from a higher calling," Otto said.

Reflective on the time spent during the past few hours, Camila said, "I can't imagine how painful it must be to live life with the wrong identity just because you have the wrong biological makeup. It makes you wonder why some people are created with the gender they feel is wrong."

"I would never have guessed about Miller," Martin said. He was still a little bewildered.

"I've had several students who've gone through gender reassignment," Linda said.

"I wonder how a God can put a person into a body they feel is flawed and needs to be altered surgically," Camila replied.

"Gender issues are unbelievably complex and mysterious," Otto said. "Isn't that right, Doctor?"

THE FLAT TIRE

"Don't confuse gender with sexuality," Linda said. "They are separate."

Martin remained silent.

Eli said, "God has placed us here, male or female. I believe that's how we are intended. I know there are factors and circumstances contributing to how a person sees and identifies with their gender. I don't believe it's always about Nature. Often, it can be about events during the formative years or how your parents treat you. Jewish mystics explain that everyone has both feminine and masculine elements. Even with behavior, there are feminine aspects to a man and masculine aspects to a woman. I don't believe it's a simple matter for someone to go ahead and say, 'I'm definitely not a man' or 'I'm definitely not a woman,' even though biologically, they were born that way. You may be tampering with something that may not bring you happiness. It's not simple. Anyone in a healthy relationship with their sexuality will know they have aspects of the opposite gender. I say this with the sensitivity that a person can be dealing with distortions of how to perceive their sexuality. I think you'd agree, Doctor, that we live in a world where gender identity is a mess?"

Linda was tolerating what Eli was saying but dying to correct him on several of his misconceptions. She chose silence.

"Heterosexuals, homosexuals, and all the other names and titles exist because sexuality has become divorced from intimacy. I see sexuality as often separate from purpose and viewed as personal pleasure. Some people feel proud to say,

'I'm in a sexual relationship without commitment.' Tell me, is that healthy intimacy?"

Eli didn't wait for an answer and continued, "On the other hand, there are profound experiences that aren't just sexual. I believe people must understand their soul to discover their life's purpose. You may change something and then discover you're not happier simply because you never took the time to find out your calling. Every male and every female has a calling and a mission. It's critical to embrace one's mission. When you're at peace with that, then your gender fits right in. Because your gender is part of how you fulfill the purpose and calling of your life, it's critical when it comes to gender challenges that a person speaks with someone they trust – a mentor or a friend. This issue is bound up with isolation, despair, and loneliness. It's challenging to make decisions under those circumstances."

"For people my age, I wouldn't try to say all that in one of your edibles," Camila said.

"Rabbi, I think your martini has just been shaken and not stirred!" Linda said. "You're trying too hard to simplify the problem and, in doing so, have concluded that anyone grappling with identity issues is a nut job! You're being utterly irresponsible."

"Can you say that to him?" Camila asked.

"I think we've been given the all-clear to leave the lobby," Martin said.

TEEHEE

THE LAW OFFICES OF MOYTOY, BISSOUMA, PORRO, SON, AND Postecoglou were housed in a building across the street from the hotel and the remnants of the surreal chaos lingering along F Street between Fourteenth and Fifteenth. The air smelled not of spring's sweet magnolias or the early autumn's breeze but of the unfortunate. Fresh strips of crime scene tape intertwined with the vigilant stance of traffic cones created a barrier of closure extending up and down Fifteenth Street for two blocks on either side of F Street. While the boundaries of demarcation held sway against the ingress of unauthorized vehicles, an intriguing phenomenon was not lost on the officials laboring within the marked scene. A lingering plume of odors held steadfast and failed to dissipate into the ether. A common passing thought attributed the paradox to a higher power crying, "Forget-me-not."

Forced to go around the blockade instead of directly

across the street, Camila's party stayed close and walked in silence. Distant sounds of a living city funneled through the low-lying canyons between the buildings and elevated a sense of apprehension. Muscles tensed whenever a siren reverberated. Nervousness entered their stride and the desire to return inside took hold.

Being forced to acquiesce to happenstance and the inability to assert control chiseled away at Otto's gut. He couldn't find any enlightenment in the unpredictability of the morning. His phone heralded the arrival of a text with a vibration. This missive bore the insignia of his subscription to a daily wellspring of motivation, a beacon for rough seas. Captivated by the promise of hope, he yielded and unlocked the app to unveil its pearl of wisdom: "Whatever the present moment contains, accept it as if you had chosen it – Eckhart Tolle." The sentiment was met not with enthusiasm but with a quirked eyebrow and a head shake. The phone was placed back inside his jacket's jetted pocket as if to seek solace in the dark.

Traversing the threshold into the serenity of the office building's lobby, Camila detached from the tumultuous events of the morning and, without effort, metamorphosed to the here and now. She returned to her effervescent, naïve self and refocused on completing her mission to deliver everyone for their meeting.

"We'll need to go through the security magnetometer. Keys, iPads, and bags will be X-rayed. The stone on the walls and floor is called Calacatta Oro. It comes all the way from the Apuan Alps in Italy. I love how the gold veins pop

THE FLAT TIRE

from the creamy white backdrop. Michelangelo used this marble. I'm hoping to go to Italy one day. After we've collected your badges, we can go up in Ms. Moytoy's private elevator, which is just off to the right." Looking at the solitary security guard, she said, "Good morning, Ernesto. I've four guests to get signed in. They've all been preregistered."

The elevator opened up to a reception area. Martin was the first to comment as they stepped off the elevator, "Have they left any wood in the Amazon?"

The receptionist responded, "It's a fabricated faux Koa wood panel. The firm takes pride in being ecologically minded. The building is also certified platinum as a healthy, efficient, and cost-saving green building." Looking at Camila, the receptionist told her to take everyone to Teehee and that Ms. Moytoy would join them shortly. "May I get anyone tea, coffee, water?"

Teehee was the name of the firm's largest conference room. The center table heralded a matching faux Koa veneer. Twenty-four oversized office chairs with tall backs were each wrapped in soft vegan leather made from agricultural waste products and sustainable biomaterials. The twin entrance doors bore the same faux Koa and were flanked by floor-to-ceiling glass walls on either side. The electrically operated stark white Venetian-style blinds were closed to prevent anyone from looking in or out. The sterile white had been chosen for the Cherokee association for peace and happiness. The far side of the room was windowed with a view of Fourteenth Street and a building that housed a foreign national bank specializing in international payments, letters of credit services, and import and export documentary collection services. The two windowless side walls were adorned with framed facsimiles of enlightenment and tragedy. Each piece was delicately reproduced on aesthetically aged, museum-quality parchment and encased in wide, ordinate, gilded frames with conservation glazing to eliminate the ultraviolet that leads to fading. History was not merely on display. It was being enshrined.

The curated facsimiles included the Declaration of Independence and the Thirteenth Amendment. A lesser-known aspect of the amendment was it only addressed 87.5% of the enslaved Africans. Other works included the Civil Rights Act of 1964 next to General Order Number Three, a document corresponding to the annual Juneteenth celebration. The four prints on the opposing wall included Article Seven from the Treaty of New Echota. The next pair of prints, *Roe versus Wade* and *Dobbs versus Jackson Women's Health Organization* spoke to women's issues. The Roe print showcased definition twelve: the "Word 'person' as used in the Fourteenth Amendment does not include the unborn." Dobbs focused on footnote fourteen, "The Act defines 'gestational age' to be 'the age of an unborn human being as calculated from the first day of the last menstrual period of the pregnant woman.'" The final print was The Respect for Marriage Act, which provided the narrative for section two.

Below the four prints, a long console table hugged the wall with eleven evenly distributed photographic frames.

THE FLAT TIRE

Each one contained a different copy of each Congressional declaration of war, from the 1812 declaration against Great Britain to the 1942 declaration against Romania. Conspicuously absent was the one thing everyone expected to see: a towering wall adorned with an array of law books. From its inception, the firm adopted a policy to be digital-first and as paperless as possible.

Camila asked everyone to sit and excused herself. "I've enjoyed meeting y'all. I mean, despite the event of this morning."

Camila exited. Before the door closed, a man with a distinguished air of a high-powered, seasoned attorney entered. Yves Bissouma was in his late fifties and a man who was as overbearing as the scent from his aftershave. Each thread of his meticulously tailored navy pinstriped suit paid homage to the principle of exactitude. It reflected his adherence to precision in thought, attire, and expectation. The crimson hue of his bow tie, resplendent like a cardinal standing on a snow-covered lawn, provided a harmonious contrast that evoked the echo of timeless sophistication. Every fold and contour of his ensemble, akin to the chapters of a scholarly tome, spoke of a man who reveled in the elegance of orderliness, both in the legal realm and in the sartorial fabrics gracing his form.

"Good afternoon, I'm Yves Bissouma, one of the senior partners here at Moytoy, Bissouma, Porro, Son, and Postecoglou. I'm not staying for the meeting, but I wanted to take a moment to introduce myself and to see that you're all comfortable." Without waiting for a response, he continued, "I saw it all. I even have it on video. My suite is on the other side of the floor, and I just happened to be videoing the marchers for my daughter. She's a doctoral candidate at Howard pursuing Political Science. I thought it might be of interest to her. Truly, I found myself caught up in the vibrancy of the signs and costumes. And then, bam, the unthinkable. A car flew by like a bat out of hell. Bodies went up, under, over. Sheer tragedy. To be very honest, my brain couldn't absorb what was happening in real time. It was completely mind-numbing to experience. I realized I had captured the driver when I watched everything back. The video showed the driver getting out of the car and removing a crash helmet. There's no question this wasn't an unfortunate accident. Clearly, it was all premeditated, one hundred percent. The driver appeared a little shaken getting out of the car, but let's face it, who wouldn't be coming to a dead stop at that speed? Whoever this monster – this harbinger of chaos – was able to merge in with the crowd that didn't know which way was up or how to get out. I have a friend at the Bureau, Cammy. She's a field agent. So, I WhatsApp'd the video to her as soon as I saw what I had. Hopefully, it has enough detail to identify the malefactor. It's the latest model, so hopefully, the camera lives up to the clarity hype they've been advertising. I'm still shaking. See. Can I get anybody refreshments? I think Sequoia will be only in another minute. She's just wrapping up a Zoom session with members of the Senate Subcommittee on Human Rights."

He left the room without waiting for an answer on the beverages or a reaction to his soliloquy.

"Is anything happening outside?" Otto asked. Linda was sitting on the side of the table facing the window. Although put off by the question, she got up and walked to the window to look down on Fourteenth Street.

"It looks like the world's still in one piece."

The conference room door opened; it was the receptionist. She pushed a tea cart under the Declaration of Independence. "I've brought some bottled water, hot water for tea, and coffee. We only have regular, no decaf I'm afraid. There's milk, cream, lemon slices, depending on your preference, and a broad selection of tea bags. There's also a bowl with real sugar." She left the room, closing the door behind her.

"I could do with some strong black coffee," Otto said. But before he could get up, the door opened again, and in walked two gentlemen.

"Good afternoon. We thought we'd just pop in to say that we appreciate you coming in today. I'm Pedro Porro, and this is Ange Postecoglou. We're both senior partners at the firm. Ange is a retired colonel and was internal counsel for the Department of Defense. Because of the late start, we won't be able to sit in, but Ms. Moytoy should be by any minute. I believe she's just wrapping up a Zoom session with members of the Senate Subcommittee on Human Rights. Lunch will arrive soon. The Hamilton, the restaurant downstairs, provides an exquisite spread, and everyone's usually satisfied with their quality. I see that our receptionist has provided refreshments, but is there anything else I can bring for anybody?"

No one spoke.

It was Ange's turn. "In that case if you'll excuse us. We'll see you later on."

"This merry-go-round is a little disturbing," Martin said. "They're still being rather nondescript about the exact nature of the meeting. And they're treating us like we're an imposition. I'm sorry, Linda, may I impose on you to grab me a bottle of water? I'm feeling a little woozy."

"Geronimo's changed course again," Otto said. His head was buried in his phone. "The forecast has it hugging the coastline all the way to Cape Cod before heading out into the Atlantic. The outer bands should encroach on our area soon. We'll likely see some mild to heavy rain, even a flash flood. They might be getting ready to close Reagan and Dulles."

Linda rose gracefully from her seat and sauntered over to the drink trolley. Her fingers plucked the nearest bottle of water. It seemed as if, in this gathering of men, she had unwittingly assumed the role of the maid. The notion was beginning to gnaw at her patience. Returning to the table where Martin sat, she set the bottle before him with an air of subtle sarcasm. Her voice, tinged with irony, slipped past undetected as she inquired, "Shall I do the honors and open it for you?"

"Yes, thank you, Linda."

Eli's fingers began a rhythmic dance on the tabletop, a silent expression of his growing impatience for Sequoia to

THE FLAT TIRE

appear. He realized his tapping produced no audible resonance on the faux wood. He couldn't resist a playful comment delivered with a sly grin, "Seems this imitation wood lacks both timber and timbre, doesn't it? Get it?"

Linda's patience reached its boiling point. "It's hardly surprising that none of you ever married," she said. Realizing the need to regain her composure, she paused briefly, "Excuse me for a moment; I'm just going to use the ladies' room."

Wanting to establish peace, Otto responded right away. He stood up and began moving toward the door, "Please allow me to get the door for you."

"Don't patronize me, Cardinal. I'm not in the mood."

No sooner had Linda left the room to find the bathroom than Sequoia made her appearance. Rushing in, she didn't take time to read the room, "I'm so, so sorry. I was on a call with members from the Senate Subcommittee for Human Rights, and they just kept going on and on. Senators and the President, it's difficult to hang up on these people. I'm Sequoia Moytoy." She looked, "Oh, I see we're missing one!"

"Doctor Herzog will be right back. She excused herself for a moment," Otto said.

The light in the room changed subtly; raindrops began sprinkling on the windowpane. "Looks like Geronimo has arrived," Sequoia said. "Lunch should be arriving soon." Pausing to breathe, she continued. "Thank you all for coming today. The events this morning, well, nothing short of harrowing. One of our partners managed to capture everything on his phone. I saw the playback, let me tell you, it was utterly gut-wrenching. We've sent the footage over to the FBI. Hopefully, it'll lead them to who did this. The actual incident unfolded in the literal blink of an eye. But the repercussions were immediate and heartbreaking. Witnessing all of these people being flung into the air like paper dolls. It was a sobering reminder of how swiftly life can change."

Sequoia glanced at the window. "I'm grateful that our windows are soundproof, sparing us from the hysteria below. I was in my office when it occurred, so I didn't see or hear anything. One of my associates came and told me. I went to one of my partner's offices, which has a good view of the street, and he was still videoing the situation. I looked down at the aftermath and could barely catch my breath. After he stopped recording, he played everything back for me. You must have heard everything at the hotel. I think I recollect seeing Imam Martin on the video giving some poor soul CPR. Your courage and quick action were commendable, a shining example of doing the right thing in the face of adversity."

She took a moment to look harder at Martin. "Are you feeling alright? You're looking a little iffy."

"I'm fine, thank you, Ms. Moytoy. It's been a busy day, and I think I'm just a little fatigued and, perhaps, a little lightheaded."

The conference room door reopened, and Linda entered. "Ah, Doctor Herzog, is everything alright? I'm Sequoia Moytoy. I'm so glad you're all here. Please take a seat."

Sequoia sat at the head of the table. Behind her was the tea and coffee. The Declaration of Independence on the wall behind her surrounded her head like a halo.

"Thank you all for coming. As I've mentioned, I'm Sequoia Moytoy, and it's a pleasure to meet you, Cardinal LaMacchia, Imam Martin, Doctor Herzog, and Rabbi Rahabi. Under the circumstances, I'm even more appreciative of your being here. I recognize much of my email communication with you was intentionally nebulous. But we're working very hard to keep things close to the chest at the moment and not running the risk of too much information being leaked."

"Yes, we uncovered over breakfast that we were all being kept in the dark, so to speak," Otto said.

"My practice has become renowned for human rights and constitutional law. We operate in fourteen countries worldwide, and while we will take on other cases, we have our sweet spot. Some people in this country with deep pockets have approached us to help with some remediation."

"What does that mean?" Eli asked.

"It was all part of the briefing I was in. We want to put forth a Redeclaration of Independence for the United States."

"A what?"

"A Redeclaration of Independence."

"You mean like renewing your marriage vows?"

"No. The intent is to correct and modernize the original Declaration so that equality, equity, and justice for all are far less ambiguous and much less prone to reinterpretation. Renewing your vows doubles down on what already has been agreed upon. This is about change. Change for the better. Recalibrating our North Star."

"Language is fragile and always evolving," Eli said. "Will a Redeclaration solve the etymology issues over time? It's why, in Judaism, we have the Talmud. It's a separate document from the Torah that helps elaborate on language and meaning by providing an explanation with room for new insights to be incorporated. It mitigates us from rewriting anything. Are you sure you want to redraft the Declaration of Independence? That doesn't seem right."

"Why are we here?" Linda asked.

"What about the Constitution?" Otto asked.

"We'll get to all of your questions," Sequoia said.

"Go on," Martin said.

"The Declaration of Independence comes from a time and a place where people declared what they were against. In our modern times, there are those who want to pursue a declaration based on what people are for and built on a platform of equality, equity, and justice," Sequoia said.

"And acceptance and belonging, too," Linda said.

"A minute ago, you used the word 'we,'" Eli said. "You went on to say, 'We want to put forth.' I assume this endeavor is a little more personal. Perhaps your vested interest in this matter has extended beyond the scope of a significant retainer. Are you willing to share your personal angle in all of this?"

"I thought this might come up later," Sequoia said. "But

okay. I am fully aware the Declaration of Independence, hanging behind me, is one of the three founding documents of this nation. It's a document signed by fifty-six of the Founding Fathers. But as an indigenous person, the term Founding Father is a little too generous. It's a perversion of revisionist history. From where I sit, I stare at another document, the Treaty of New Echota. A document signed in 1835 on behalf of the United States of America and the *Ani-Yun-Wiya*, the Cherokee Nation. I'm reminded of the reneged and unfulfilled legal obligations, to this very day, by our federal government whenever I sit in this chair."

Sequoia began reciting the article from memory, "The Cherokee nation having already made great progress in civilization and deeming it important that every proper and laudable inducement should be offered to their people to improve their condition as well as to guard and secure in the most effectual manner the rights guaranteed to them in this treaty, and with a view to illustrate the liberal and enlarged policy of the Government of the United States towards the Indians in their removal beyond the territorial limits of the States, it is stipulated that they shall be entitled to a delegate in the House of Representatives of the United States whenever Congress shall make provision for the same."

"Which means what exactly?"

"For centuries, my people have been denied the rightful place they were promised in the House of Representatives. This conference room is named for Kimberly Teehee. She's the Cherokee Nation's delegate-designate, our representative waiting to take her rightful seat. This promise, enshrined in a treaty without an expiration date, continues to be disregarded. While the Declaration of Independence eloquently proclaims that 'all men are created equal,' we cannot ignore the language of Article Seven, which implies the indigenous peoples in 1776 were not considered equal. A similar case can be made for enslaved Africans, as the language of the Declaration is squarely rooted in the grievances of a handful of angry white men against a perceived oppressor. We firmly believe a Redeclaration of Independence is not just necessary but long overdue. It should reflect a new order. The back of our paper money contains the Latin phrase, *Novus ordo seclorum*. It is time for a new order of the ages, one that transcends the basis of opposition to one championing a unity rooted in the values and dignity of all people, regardless of their acuity, ideology, or faith. It's time to stand for something that embraces diversity and inclusion."

"I'm feeling a little nauseous and experiencing a little abdominal pain," Martin said. "Which way is the restroom?"

LILITH

LILITH LIN CLUTCHED AT HER BLANKIE. RUBBING IT GENTLY against her nose provided some solace while she slept snuggled in her stroller. An hour had passed since her eyes closed, a duration in line with her routine for this time of day. She looked angelic and, by all appearances, appeared to be in the pinnacle of health – another normal baby girl. As a result of this pediatric visit, her mother would be confronted with the stark reality of a new normal. Much like other two-year-old children, Lilith possessed the remarkable ability to transition effortlessly between contrasting behavioral states. She could be utterly adorable and calm one minute, only to transform into a fiery toddler the next, unleashing a torrent of anguished cries that filled the air with defiance. Inside Sierra Vista's lone north-side pediatrician's office, her mother rocked the baby carriage and listened to the doctor's opinions. Truth be told, her instinct had already suspected everything she heard.

"Are you still working?" the pediatrician said.

"No. Not at the moment. When Hua and I learned we were pregnant with Lilith, we decided I would be a stay-at-home mom. I think we get that from our Asian heritage."

"Well, that's really going to help."

"Let's hope!" her mother said.

According to Jewish mysticism, Eve wasn't Adam's first spouse. While Eve was *made*, his first spouse, Lilith, had been *formed*, just like him. Their brief marriage ended in a less-than-amicable separation, a marital spat about who should be on top. Lilith decided to abscond from Paradise on her own volition. Exiling herself to the depths of the outside wilderness, she chose to embrace her nature as a mother of demons, a harbinger of chaos. Eve took over the reins as Adam's ephemeral *good* wife. Lilith Lin's parents picked the name because they liked how it sounded; they would never learn about their child's worthy namesake.

"How long have you and your husband been here? Do you have a support system? Other family members, perhaps?" the pediatrician asked.

"It's been a good five years since we moved from Washington," her mother said.

"D.C.?"

"No. State. My husband grew up in Seattle. I grew up less than an hour away in Tacoma. We met in the service. We fell madly in love and got married within a year. We've been here ever since we got assigned to the Fort. Overall, we love the quiet and the close-knit community."

Not counting illegal immigrants, Sierra Vista's

population hovers around thirty-five thousand. The local cemeteries accommodate an even greater population. The town is nestled in the rugged landscapes of southeastern Arizona. When gazing skyward, it's not uncommon to spot an airborne blimp diligently maintaining a constant watch for would-be drug runners. The brochures of the area frequently brim with undeniable propaganda, extolling the virtues of a quality of life that supposedly surpasses the norm. It paints a picture of an experience characterized by the seamless blend of "desert tranquility" and "small-town charm." Narratives tell of an unfolding backdrop of majestic mountains and endless skies while leaving out details about the clear and present dangers of frequent visits from potentially hostile outsiders. Without the steadfast presence of the United States government, Sierra Vista would likely have faded into obscurity decades ago, becoming another victim of the wild west, another ghost town.

Fort Huachuca is the hub of employment and provides the area with economic viability. The base is home to the United States Army Intelligence Center of Excellence. Its primary mission is developing military intelligence professionals. Additionally, the base accommodates numerous other units with lengthy and confusing military acronyms. Overall, Fort Huachuca is critical in supporting national security interests through various intelligence, communications, and cybersecurity missions.

Lilith's parents were both of Asian American descent. Her father, Hua, was in his early forties and ran the garrison command. In the annals of history, the garrison had been assigned to the famous Buffalo Soldiers. Today, the garrison command is essential in overseeing infrastructure operations and services. Her mother, Sunoo, had been a commissioned officer assigned to an intelligence unit within the fort. She retired from active service after her second trimester.

The fort's history dates back to the era of cowboys and Indians. Its claim to fame is its origin as the birthplace of the Army's policy of awarding three days of leave for an enlisted soldier – the time off provided for rest and relaxation. In the days when riding horseback was the dominant mode of transportation, soldiers were given a day to ride to Tombstone and a day to ride back. The middle day was reserved for outright debauchery.

The word "Huachuca" is derived from the language of the Apache Indians and means "place of thunder." The original military outpost was tasked with protecting settlers and travelers and transitioned into a base for conducting operations against bands of hostile Apache Indians led by Cochise and Geronimo. The Fort's use as a genocide camp has long been swept under the rug. In 1882, Camp Huachuca was designated as a permanent military installation due to its strategic location near the U.S.-Mexico border and its role in maintaining regional security and stability. The post expanded and evolved over the years to accommodate changing needs and technological advancements, particularly in the field of military intelligence.

History has given Geronimo the immutable status of a

legendary Apache warrior. His name is synonymous with courage and resistance in the face of adversity. Born into a world steeped in tradition and ancestral lore, Geronimo emerged as a formidable figure, revered for his prowess in battle and his unwavering commitment to defend Apache lands against encroaching settlers and military incursions. Incarcerated within the confines of Fort Huachuca, Geronimo found himself ensnared in the web of colonial expansion and territorial ambition.

Geronimo and his band had waged relentless guerrilla campaigns against the U.S. Army, whose mission was to subdue the Apache resistance. Through cunning tactics and unmatched knowledge of the terrain, Geronimo evaded capture time and again, earning him a reputation as a wily antagonist and a symbol of defiance. Despite his valiant efforts, he ultimately surrendered. The decision was not borne out of defeat but out of pragmatism. He wanted to spare his people further bloodshed. He became a prisoner of war. His once-proud spirit was tempered by shackles. Yet, even in the torrents of despair, his indomitable spirit remained unbroken.

In fifth grade, Lilith was taught about the rallying cry "Geronimo." However, this lesson did not come from one of her teachers. It was from one of her friends, a young boy in the same grade with an indigenous heritage. She was told that the phrase embodied a rich history regarding Geronimo's daring exploits and willingness to defy the odds when faced with overwhelming danger.

"During one of his fearless escapes, Geronimo and his

men leaped from one cliff to another," the boy said. "In Geronimo's desperate bid for freedom, they all flew through the air like Spider-Man and shouted 'Ger-on-i-mooo.' We call that a rallying cry, and it still serves as a symbol for my people's courage and defiance."

Back in the pediatrician's office, Sunoo was told, "We'll need to perform some additional tests, but Lilith is showing signs of Autism Spectrum Disorder. She's autistic."

"Honestly, I've been afraid of that," Sunoo said. "Lily's lack of interest in interacting with us has been causing me concern. I've always felt her unwillingness to make eye contact was a tale-tale sign. Honestly, it's what prompted my initial visit."

"She has some delayed language skills. That's associated with her not wanting to imitate some of the sounds you make when playing with her," the pediatrician said.

"Is this why we see her continually lining up her Barbie and GI-Joe dolls? I can't believe how intensely focused she can be at times."

"Indeed. You'll likely notice that even more and more. Lilith may have times of intense or focused interest in particular topics, objects, or activities. But you should be careful about her sensitivity to certain sounds, textures, or lights while in the throes of an activity. She may also seek sensory stimulation by engaging in repetitive behaviors."

"I mentioned earlier that I had planned to be a stay-at-home mom. I should be able to keep her in a routine to avoid unnecessary transitions or changes if that helps?"

"Good, good. You should also know that some of Lilith's

THE FLAT TIRE

playtime may not show signs of imagination. Stay alert, paying attention to learn how she engages. As a tip, try to keep any objects or toys that she's formed an attachment with close by. Let me see you both back in six months. I'm sorry I didn't have better news for you. Have a nice day."

"Yes. Thank you, doctor."

In later years, based on her developmental history, behavioral observations, and other standardized assessments, Lilith's condition was redefined as high-functioning ASD. One aspect she enjoyed with unusual enthusiasm was working alongside her father in his shop. The family's three-bedroom, two-bath, ranch-style home had an attached three-car garage. The family's runaround was a three-row Kia SUV, which occupied the garage stall nearest the front door. The other two stalls held Hua's material pride-and-joy: his split-window Corvette and Pontiac GTO muscle car. The GTO's provenance even had a photograph of John DeLorean sitting behind the wheel. Hua's shop was a prefabricated metal barn located behind the house. It took up most of the backyard. He had a vast array of greasy automotive equipment and kept his historic vehicles in pristine working order. He'd earned a reputation for his automotive skills within the local community. Many of the soldiers assigned to the fort would bring their cars to him to eke out extra horsepower.

For some reason, Lilith never found the smell of grease off-putting, and her father was always careful to avoid inadvertently letting his tools clank. By age fourteen, Barbie had long been forgotten and left behind in the desert sand. Lilith had become skilled at helping her father.

One spring weekend morning, her father brought the Corvette into the workshop. "Lilith, it's time for the Stingray to get a tune-up. Do you have time to help out your dad?"

She clapped with glee and her eyes lit up with excitement. She always jumped at the chance to ride in the Corvette with her father. With the hood open and the car turned on, she could watch the Rochester fuel-injected engine visibly oscillate. For some reason, she enjoyed staring at it.

"Lilith, did you know that this engine is older than the both of us?" Hua asked. "The Rochester Ramjet fuel injection system consists of three main components. This part here is the air meter, this is the fuel meter, and this right here is what is called the intake manifold. Now, what makes this an extra special engine is that, when it was born, it passed the threshold of one horsepower per cubic inch of engine displacement. Back then, that was a notable accomplishment."

Lilith might not have comprehended every word, but the radiant smile she beamed filled Hua's heart with warmth and joy. They set to work with tools in hand and a sense of determination. Hua had developed a nurturing trait of patience to help his daughter and prepared her for when a loud sound might occur, even though she wore noise-canceling headphones. She stood by his side while he carefully adjusted the carburetor and checked the spark plugs, handing him tools and offering suggestions whenever she spotted something she thought was amiss. When it came to the exterior workings of an engine, Lilith developed a keen eye for detail and a natural talent for understanding.

"I'm still trying to make my way through all of this medical literature," Sunoo said.

"To be honest, much of it is going over my head," Hua said.

"It says in this paper that 'Among all of the intricate neurodevelopmental disorders, ASD remains a captivating enigma.' And here, it goes on to say, 'The delicate interplay of genetics, biology, and environmental factors that have intertwined to form its complexity.' I really wish there was something more that we could do."

"I'm sure medical science will come up with something."

"This part says, 'It's defined by a constellation of symptoms encompassing challenges in social interaction, communication, and repetitive behaviors. Autism can stymie many of those working in the field. At its core, autism manifests as a divergence from typical patterns of brain development, with alterations in neural connectivity, neurotransmitter function, and neuroanatomy contributing to its complex phenotype.' That just means the observable physical properties. 'Within the machinations of the autistic brain, the balance between excitatory and inhibitory neurotransmission teeters on a precipice, shaping the intricacies between sensory processing, emotion regulation, and cognitive flexibility,'" Sunoo said.

"I'm hopeful that she'll be fine," Hua said.

With encouragement and support from her parents, Lilith enlisted in the U.S. Air Force when she turned eighteen. She was assigned to the Davis-Monthan Air Force Base. Her parents were delighted because the base was located on the outskirts of Tucson and was less than an hour's drive away from their home. The base stores thousands of military and commercial aircraft because of the area's rust-free environment, thanks to a severe absence of rain and the low desert humidity.

Lilith was assigned to the base's automobile workshop and was surrounded by many large machines she'd never seen before. Her task was reasonably straightforward: maintaining the fleet of jeeps and other vehicles that military personnel used daily to carry out their job functions. At first, a few of her colleagues were skeptical. A young woman with autism working in a male-dominated field – several raised doubts but chose to temper their voices and opinions. Armed with her self-belief, her steadfast determination, and her unwavering passion for mechanics, she was not distracted. No one understood exactly why, but her favorite activity in the workshop was fixing flat tires.

For ten years, she flourished. Being close to Sierra Vista meant her parents visited her often. Home-cooked pasta on Friday nights became a family tradition and offered comfort for everyone, emotionally and physically – especially when satiated. Her parents would each drink a glass of Cabernet Sauvignon. Lilith drank Coke through a straw. Despite her talents and contributions, several factors within the context of her employer limited her opportunities for advancement and progression. One significant challenge faced by individuals with ASD is the established culture of the Air Force's rigid hierarchy and its emphasis on conformity. The branch operates on a strict chain of command, where adherence to rules, regulations, and self-imposed norms is required. Lilith's occasional struggles with social interactions, communication, and flexibility meant navigating the hierarchical structure was daunting. For anyone suffering from her type of debilitating condition, understanding and adhering to protocols and norms can be a hindrance to advancement in rank or in assuming leadership roles.

Her superiors within the mechanical workshop were compassionate. They took measures to shield her from the demanding and occasionally fast-paced work, which had the potential to heighten her stress and anxiety levels. Her supervisors made every effort to maintain a predictable workload. During her annual review, she was informed about an opening at Joint Base Andrews in Maryland, situated near Washington, D.C. Her parents were invited to Davis-Monthan and consulted about the opportunity for their daughter. By the end of the meeting, everyone was in agreement, and preparations commenced.

To get Lilith settled at Andrews, her mother traveled with her and stayed for the better part of two months. Toward the end of her visit, Lilith received a three-day pass. Her mother decided they would take a short trip to the capital and tour some of the monuments and museums.

Their first stop was the majestic Lincoln Memorial, with a lone statue and towering columns. Sunoo and Lilith gazed in admiration at the solemnity of the craftsmanship and their shared moment. As they made their way through the National Mall, Sunoo guided Lilith through various museums and galleries along the adjoining streets. From the awe-inspiring exhibits within the Smithsonian to the poignant memorials honoring the sacrifices of those who came before them, every step they took was imbued with appreciation and the joy of sharing this precious time together. One of their most memorable stops was the National Air and Space Museum. On display was a replica of a lunar vehicle used during NASA's early missions to the moon. Lilith's fascination seemed to soar. By late afternoon, mother and daughter walked past the White House and stood in front of the Treasury Building. Sunoo looked across the street and saw a restaurant, The Hamilton.

"Let's go there and get something to eat and drink," she said.

Another year passed, and Lilith even acquired a driver's license. She passed Maryland's assessment on her ability to meet requirements and demonstrate safe driving skills. Soon after, a colleague told her about a Tesla Plaid for sale. It had been in an accident, and the owner wanted to offload the vehicle because he thought it was bad luck and hadn't bothered to try to get anything fixed. The damage wasn't too bad. Lilith even gained permission from the base to remediate the bodywork in the base's facilities. Afterward, she sent her car to a nearby commercial auto body and paint facility to get repainted. She chose black.

Lilith was acutely aware of the challenges of working at Andrews. As a high-functioning autistic woman, she knew she would face a new round of skepticism and prejudice from some of her peers. She remained undeterred, fueled by a fierce patriotism and a desire to prove herself worthy.

Her mental unraveling began soon after she had made friends with a group of three women aged between twenty-five and forty-two. The women worked in aircraft maintenance as civilian employees. Two of them were electricians; the other, the older woman, was a pneudraulics expert. One evening, Lilith was invited to join them for dinner at a quiet and low-key bar in nearby Forestville. It's difficult for a woman, any woman, to protect herself when she becomes a target of the group she's associated with. It was the younger woman who chose to pour ketamine into Lilith's glass of Coca-Cola after she'd gotten up to use the restroom.

Ketamine is odorless, colorless, and tasteless when placed in a drink. Other popular date-rape drugs, such as Gamma-Butyrolactone, can have a bitter flavor. But even that can be masked if put into something strong-tasting.

About fifteen minutes after Lilith returned from the restroom, the women asked for the check. They left with Lilith to go to their vehicle. Shortly after, Lilith passed out, and the four women drove to a seedy, cash-only motel in Morningside. Lilith – in and out of consciousness – began experiencing a strange feeling of detachment from her body and surroundings.

"I'm really not feeling myself. Can we go home," Lilith said.

During the assault in room 107, she had no real idea or reference point as to what was happening but knew something was wrong. Thanks to the ketamine, she was unable to move or fight back.

"If she's lucky, she'll remember how fun this all was and won't suffer from amnesia," the older woman said.

"Should we just leave her here?"

"Let her sleep it off. Housekeeping will find her in the morning. Let's go."

When Lilith woke, she instinctively felt something was wrong and couldn't understand where she was. Like many victims, she had been physically helpless, unable to refuse sex, and unable to remember exactly what happened. Alone and vulnerable, Lilith had found herself with the aircraft maintenance workers, who saw in her autism not an equal but a target of opportunity. In the darkness of the motel room, she was subjected to unspeakable acts. Unable to plead for mercy, her attackers reveled in their cruelty.

When Lilith reported to her superiors that she thought something was amiss, she was met with disbelief and indifference. Her accusations were dismissed as the ravings of a troubled mind. As the weeks turned into months, she found herself sinking deeper and deeper into an abyss of despair. The weight of shame and humiliation borne out by her confusion eroded her sense of self-worth.

THE FLAT TIRE

Lilith set about working on her Tesla without an overt sense of premeditation. She located and removed the vehicle identification numbers for an unclear reason. She started by removing the stamped number from the plate atop the dashboard. Next, she found the product plate located on the front passenger door. From there, she hoisted the car on a lift and removed the stamped number from the chassis under the sill panel. With two locations left, she systematically removed the number from the center pillar inside the driver's door and, finally, the label attached to the rear hatch. Her car was now deidentified. She remained unclear as to why her actions were important.

Isolated within the throngs of a busy base, Lilith was suffering from post-traumatic stress disorder and found within her an urge to make amends for the unquantifiable wrongs she felt had been done to her. It was a wrong that she could neither articulate nor identify. The vehicles she worked on required mechanical attention to operate properly; she wasn't getting the psychological help she needed to function. Mentally, she was broken – and fully embodying the spirit of her namesake. In due course, she took the Tesla on a twenty-mile journey. The interim destination was a parking spot in a garage on F Street in Washington, D.C.

EQUALITY

Martin stared at himself, trying to take stock of his inner state. His arms extended with both hands pushed down on the countertop edge, which allowed him to balance and fully engage with the reflection coming back off the expansive mirror. The office bathroom was resplendent when compared to other such facilities. The lighting was pleasant to the eye, bright but not glaring. The color palate was cued from a jade green. All floor and wall surfaces were eco-friendly and easy to keep sanitary. To the right of the entrance door were three white porcelain urinals with automatic flushers and two stalls with security and privacy panels also constructed from eco-friendly materials. On the opposing wall to the entrance was a janitor's closet. To the left were two, under-mount ramp sinks surrounded by a high-quality dark jade-colored stone resin. Each sink was just over four feet in width. Each featured two sets of faucets with an ultra-low flow rate to make them favorites of the Environmental Protection Agency.

Martin stared at himself with increased intensity. *I've had intense thoughts about Kalima since her passing,* he thought. *But they never resulted in such penetrating feelings like this. It's as if the Universe conspired to present me with a captivating revelation. I swear the waitress' eyes were unmistakably familiar. I've gazed into those same eyes a thousand times, and every time, I've endlessly lost all sense of time and space. This must be irrefutable evidence of the soul's existence, a profound spiritual reconnection to my Kalima. It was as though those eyes I saw today got into my psyche and spoke to me. Whatever she said has roused and awakened elements of passion I have long repressed. Remarkably, her name mirrored that of Kalima's – a synchronicity too uncanny to dismiss as a coincidence. It's not the same name, true, but it's practically identical. And then... Miller. While I may have been momentarily taken aback by what unfolded before me, the revelation of her birth name has also perplexed me. What is getting me so rattled? Why now? I just need to settle down and find serenity in this moment. Take a few deep breaths. This is the anniversary of my beloved Kalima's passing, a day that always bears heavy significance in my heart. But I have been able to honor her memory through all of the previous anniversaries. It's not like I ever forget about her. Perhaps this fatigue and dizziness will pass soon. This abdominal discomfort will eventually dissipate. It's probably nothing more than a bout of indigestion or gas. I'll try using the restroom stall again. But just to be safe, I'd better make a call first.*

Back in the conference room, while they waited for

Martin's return, Eli took a position. "I believe that in colonial times, the word 'men' had a broader meaning. I don't believe it was used in a way that limited it to males. I think it was a term intended to encompass all human beings, regardless of gender."

"Rabbi, it isn't that straightforward. When Jefferson penned the immortal words, 'all men are created equal,' he wasn't referring to individual equality. Prominent legal and academic scholars argue the Continental Congress primarily sought the right to statehood rather than emphasizing individual liberties. In its historical context, this phrase wasn't meant to signify personal equality. Instead, the colonists were boldly asserting their right to self-governance as a united people, collectively and within each state, positioning themselves on par with other nations. This was the essence of its original intent. Only in the decades following the Revolutionary War did the phrase evolve into a cornerstone of individual equality," Sequoia said.

"Sure, the Declaration of Independence serves as a foundational document outlining principles upon which our government and our identity as Americans are technically built," Linda said. "And it is distinct from the other founding documents in that it lacks any legal enforceability. So, I'm not sure there's really any type of question for us to address in your pursuit."

"I would concur with Doctor Herzog," Eli said. "I don't see why we would need a Redeclaration even if 'human being' or some other generic phrase was substituted for 'men.'"

"Thank you," Linda said.

"However, I would think we might want to examine the word 'equal' and explore what 'equality' truly entails," Eli said. "From where I sit, I observe a world where people are unequal in various aspects of life. Some hold positions of authority. Some hold sickening amounts of wealth. I was once in that dilemma. Power dynamics vary, and leadership qualities are not universally distributed. We must look at intelligence, too. It differs from person to person; we accept this by measuring aptitude and I.Q. However, diversity exists without an implication of superiority. As individuals, we all possess distinct qualities and attributes that set us apart – everything from our physical appearance to our opinions and thought processes to our distinct personalities. No two identical individuals exist in this world; we are all unique. Therefore, we must start with what is meant by 'equality.' Ultimately, if being equal means everything, it'll effectively mean nothing."

"Yet, the words the Founding Fathers inscribed into the Declaration of Independence laid the groundwork for the eventual abolition of slavery," Otto said.

"The Declaration itself is a point of departure," Sequoia said. "The Constitution is a set of commitments, some troubling, while others were transformative. The Declaration, in its concision, gives us self-evident truths. The original Constitution, by contrast, involves a set of political commitments that recognized the legal status of slavery within the states and made the federal government culpable for upholding what was referred to as 'the peculiar institution.' The Constitution was deeply implicated in establishing a slaveholders' republic and the associated attitudes that impacted the indigenous peoples."

"The irony is not lost on me," Linda said. "The very individuals who crafted the Declaration of Independence were slaveholders. They didn't extend the principle of equality to all inhabitants of the colonies. It's worth noting that the Founding Fathers didn't even use the term 'men' to refer to all groups within the population."

"So, your position is that the groundwork can only be attributed to happenstance?" Otto asked. "Is not the Declaration of Independence a foundational tenet that has, in actuality, transcended considerations of color, creed, culture, race, and religion? This principle that all people are inherently equal, including women, remains integral to the document."

"Jefferson recorded some clarifying thoughts in the following years after the Declaration of Independence was signed," Sequoia said. "In one paper, he said, 'Among the Romans, emancipation required but one effort. When made free, the enslaved person might mix with, without staining, the blood of his master. But with us, a second is necessary, unknown to history. When freed, he is to be removed beyond the reach of mixture.'"

"Can you clarify what you're getting at?" Otto asked.

"While it's true Jefferson entertained thoughts that African Americans should be freed, he also wrote that they should be colonized elsewhere. If he were alive today, we'd call him a racist bigot. History is plagued with the disruptive efforts of the white man as he moved around the world. Jefferson's statement amounts to nothing more than an acknowledged mistake in bringing Africans to this land. Likewise, the land of people was stolen by the White man only to turn the land into a state park in Georgia. If you turn something into a state park, you could equally have left well alone. No historical account of the origins of American slavery and the indigenous tribes would ever satisfy our moral conscience today. Hence, it makes sense to pursue a Redeclaration."

"Martin's been gone for more than five minutes. Perhaps we should check on him," Linda said. "Where's the restroom?"

"I'll have my receptionist get someone to check." Sequoia picked up a receiver and pushed a button. Her call was immediately answered. "Could you please send one of the male associates to check on Imam Martin in the restroom? He's been gone longer than we expected. I just need to make sure all is well."

"Certainly, Ms. Moytoy," the receptionist said. "If I may, I've just received a message from The Hamilton. Lunch will be delayed by an hour. Due to the incident this morning, some of their employees haven't been able to make it to work, and this has caused an interruption in their deliveries."

Martin was still in the bathroom and was back at the sink, resting against the countertop with his hands. In his reflection, he saw beads of perspiration appear across his forehead. He noticed that his breath was starting to labor. *This is something else. This has nothing to do with Kalima*, he thought. Out of nowhere, he felt an intense ache in his shoulder. The pain immediately radiated down his left arm. Using his right hand, he reached over to grab his bicep. The pain only intensified. In that crucial moment, as the realization of what was unfolding washed over him, a vice-like grip constricted his chest, causing an unbearable tightness. His knees, robbed of strength, gave way beneath him. Sweat cascaded from his forehead like a summer downpour. His blood pressure plummeted, and a horrendous wave of dizziness sent the world into a disorienting spin. With a profound sense of helplessness, he crumpled to the unforgiving, unyielding floor. The ache in his arm grew more pronounced, his chest tighter, and the bathroom spun around him. A weak cry of "Allah, help me. Not now" passed his lips when the bathroom door was swung open.

Two male associates in their early thirties had been asked to check on the bathroom as they passed through the reception area on their way to lunch. They saw Martin tumble to the ground, clutching his arm. They could see the sweat dripping from his forehead and hear the shallow and sparseness of his breath. A small pool of blood appeared behind his ear.

"Call nine-one-one. Go get Ms. Moytoy. She's in Teehee with the others. I'll start CPR. It looks like a heart attack."

The associate turned and sprinted back towards the

THE FLAT TIRE

reception area, shouting to the receptionist to call the paramedics and to get an ambulance. Imam Martin needed immediate medical attention. "He's probably had a heart attack." Without stopping to provide any more color, he carried on to Teehee. The associate burst into the room without stopping to knock. His eye caught Ms. Moytoy sitting at the head of the table.

"We found Imam Martin on the floor clutching his arm. Tahoma's starting CPR. But he's also injured his head. We've called for an ambulance. I'll go back to the bathroom to help."

Sequoia picked up her telephone and dialed another number without saying a word. After two rings, the call was picked up. "This is Sequoia. I have Imam Martin at my office. We think he may have suffered a heart attack. He was feeling poorly and excused himself to go to the restroom. Yes, that's right, the Muslim leader. I know you're also a Muslim. I need a medevac here in five. Can you pull a few strings? Thank you, Mr. Speaker. Yes, I'm thinking Saint Thérèse, too. I appreciate your offer to put the hospital medical team on standby. Thank you again, Mr. Speaker."

She looked at her remaining distinguished guests and said, "The Speaker of the House is going to arrange for Imam Martin to be transported to the Cardiothoracic center at the Saint Thérèse of Lisieux Hospital in Bethesda. They have a heliport and a small adjoining runway for light aircraft. We can be assured he'll receive the best possible care no matter his condition. We have a helipad on our roof, so I've arranged to get an air ambulance, a helicopter, to transfer him. I'll conclude our meeting for today. I suggest we all head up to Bethesda. Hopefully, the EMTs won't have any trouble with Geronimo."

Otto crossed himself and prayed without invitation. "Lord, in this moment of distress and uncertainty, we place our trust in Your healing grace. We pray for Imam Martin, dear Father, that Your loving hand may guide all who treat him. Grant them strength and courage to overcome this trial. May Your divine mercy and compassion comfort Imam Martin and all of us who care deeply for their well-being. In Your holy name, we pray. Amen."

He pulled out his cell phone and began dialing. "Elrod, have you had any luck acquiring our new vehicle? Perfect. I need you to come right now and pick me up. I'll have three companions with me. We're at the office building on the corner of Fourteenth and F. It's the building across from the hotel. One moment. Yes? It'll just be an additional two passengers, not three. Ms. Moytoy will be calling for her husband to escort her. We're going to Saint Thérèse."

"I'll have our receptionist try to track the whereabouts of Martin's people," Sequoia said.

"How long before your driver is here?" Linda asked.

"He's nearby. There's not too much traffic because of the rain," Otto said.

"Which way is the restroom? I'll go and see if I can help. Do you know if you have any baby aspirin? That might help," Eli said.

Moving out into the reception area, the paramedics were already arriving. An all-female EMT crew was wheeling in a gurney on which were an oxygen tank and a defibrillator. The EMT crew was larger than normal. They were part of a multistate research program on crew sizes organized by the Inova Fairfax Hospital.

The crew could provide intravenous, intraosseous, and central line placement. They were equipped to perform an endotracheal intubation or establish a laryngeal mask airway if necessary. Each woman was determined and compassionate. They had been alerted to a possible cardiac arrest, and knew that time was of the essence. Their synchronized footsteps echoed through the corridor.

"The restroom is that way," the receptionist said without waiting for the question.

They found Martin on the floor with a small pool of blood around his head, receiving chest compressions. The EMTs took over and assessed Martin's condition.

"Pulse weak and thready... V-tach."

The machine was readied. Martin's shirt was ripped open, and the area was prepped.

"Charge to one-fifty."

The paddles were positioned.

"Charged."

"Clear."

"Still in VT. Give me two hundred. Clear!"

Martin's legs spasmed like he was dolphin kicking.

"We've got sinus. Pulse is better."

The crew loaded Martin onto the gurney and wheeled him to the elevator.

"All the way up," Sequoia said. "The helipad's on the roof."

The EMTs looked at her.

"Tahoma, go with them," Sequoia said. She looked at the lead EMT member. "I've spoken to your boss. Trust me – I've got the juice for this."

In the elevator, the paramedics continued to monitor Martin's condition, administering medications and, if necessary, poised to provide additional shocks to stabilize his heart rhythm. His vital signs weren't improving, and time was slipping away.

On the roof, Geronimo's outer band of heavy rain remained unrelenting and drenched the paramedics. As Martin transitioned from one team to the next, details were verbally given regarding his condition. With everyone onboard the helicopter, the rotator blades started to spin, and the noise pulses increased as the interactions from the tips of the rotor blades created a shed vortex. The pilot was given the all-clear, and the helicopter rose into the air and pulled away. Various messages were shared across the radio as they gained altitude and speed. Even with the torrential rain, they planned to arrive within four minutes. The O.R. and a cardiac surgery team were already standing by to deal with the left anterior descending artery blockage that the echocardiogram onboard the helicopter detected.

Meanwhile, the administrators at Saint Thérèse, bound by practice, confirmed Imam Martin's presence on their heart transplant list. Not only was he listed, but he'd also been vigilant in following protocol for maintaining his active status for readiness. Furthermore, they uncovered he'd been credentialed for a new organ at the NYC Langone Transplant Institute and the Ronald Reagan UCLA Medical Center in Los Angeles.

While Martin was being taken to the roof, a clean-shaven older gentleman strolled into the lobby of Ms. Moytoy's firm's building, his attire commanding attention. He was clad in a rich, dark brown suit adorned with a subtle broad plaid. The jacket was unbuttoned, and its length extended below the mid-thigh, lending a sense of timeless elegance with its peak lapels. His belted pleated trousers hung with a graceful, baggy drape, breaking generously over polished saddle-brown wingtip shoes that, with each step, emitted a twinkling gleam as they captured and released the ambient interior lights. Notably, he eschewed a tie, opting for a collarless plain French taupe-colored shirt that added an air of relaxed sophistication. The shirt featured abalone mother-of-pearl buttons meticulously adorning every buttoned hole, including the neck. Completing his distinctive ensemble, he wore a finely crocheted brown kufi atop his head, adding a touch of cultural richness to his overall attire. He walked with a slow, metered pace and approached the security guard.

"Excuse me. My name is Ibrahim. I received a telephone call from Imam Martin, who is attending a meeting with a law firm. He called me to collect him. He asked me to bring him to a hospital for an evaluation. I just tried calling, but he didn't answer. Please let him know I'm waiting in the lobby."

"The paramedics got here five minutes ago. They may have taken off from the roof. I'll call upstairs to confirm for you," Ernesto said just as the private elevator to Ms. Moytoy's firm opened and outstepped Sequoia, Linda, Eli, and Otto. Coincidently, Elrod entered through the lobby doors and closed his umbrella.

"One moment, Ms. Moytoy," Ernesto said. "This gentleman is here to see Imam Martin."

Everyone stopped in their tracks. Sequoia approached Ibrahim. She extended her hand to shake his hand.

"My name is Sequoia Moytoy, and you are?"

"I'm Ibrahim. I am traveling with Imam Martin, and I received a call from him a short while ago to come here and take him to a hospital. He wasn't feeling well."

"You mean it was my receptionist that called you?"

"No, ma'am. It was Imam Martin himself."

"No worries. He must have collapsed after he spoke to you. He's on his way to Saint Thérèse. The EMTs confirmed he's had some type of cardiac arrest. He's being transported in a helicopter."

"Can they fly in this weather? It's pouring outside."

"Most of the helicopters are flown by ex-military pilots. I'm sure this is just a light sprinkle compared to what they've been trained to fly through. We're all headed up to Bethesda to be with Martin. Would you like to accompany us?"

"Thank you, ma'am. I'm one of six others, and our tour bus is parked in front. I am sure we can follow you. Is the Imam going to be alright?"

THE FLAT TIRE

"Yes, yes. He's in the best possible hands. Hopefully, it'll turn out to be nothing too serious. Let me introduce you to the others. This is Cardinal LaMacchia, Doctor Herzog, and Rabbi Rahabi. And I'm sorry I didn't catch your name."

"Elrod."

"Pleasure, Elrod. Everyone, this is Ibrahim. He's been traveling with Imam Martin. Ibrahim, you can follow Elrod, who is taking everyone. My husband will be here in a few minutes. He's just wrapping up a meeting at the International Trade Center in the Ronald Reagan Building. We can all meet back up at the hospital."

GERONIMO

"Is everyone buckled? The GPS says it's just under ten miles to the hospital," Elrod said. "Hopefully, nobody got too wet."

Otto occupied the passenger seat; Eli and Linda sat in the back. When looking forward, Eli and Linda were restricted to the view of a monitor mounted into the rear of each front passenger's headrest. Both monitors were on and playing a promotional video that showcased the cabin's impressive features.

"Can we turn this off?" Linda asked.

"What's that?" Elrod asked.

"The monitors in the headrests."

"Sorry, I didn't realize those were on. I think that I can figure this out. One moment."

Elrod navigated the large touchscreen above the center console. The new SUV was an electric version of Elrod's former ride. He found the appropriate control.

THE FLAT TIRE

"Thank you," Linda said.

Elrod looked out at the street and peered into the driver's side wing mirror. The traffic was unusually light in both directions; the rain was intense. He turned on the left turn signal and pulled forward.

"Hang on," he said. "I'm going to make a U-turn. It'll be quicker."

"Ah! You've gotta love that new car smell," Eli said. "This is all very posh in here. It's much nicer than my old jalopy." *Come to think of it, I need to check with Wyclef Jean to see if my tire was replaced,* he thought. "How long have you had this?"

"A couple of hours," Elrod said.

"Really! Strange. This suspiciously sounds like you may have forgotten to share a story or two with me at breakfast, Otto?"

"All's good. Nothing to stress over. I'm just happy that Elrod has the situation in hand," Otto said.

Imam Martin's entourage in the tour bus followed Elrod's U-turn maneuver seamlessly. Fourteenth Street offered ample space for such a turn with its six-lane width and lacked the traffic volume that would have inhibited such a move on a different day. Progressing northward, the two-vehicle convoy began its journey. After a few blocks, they turned left onto H Street once the traffic light granted them passage. Windshield wipers worked tirelessly, their frantic back-and-forth motion struggling to cope with the relentless deluge.

As the convoy passed the intersection of H and Sixteenth Streets, Eli's attention was drawn to the statue of

Andrew Jackson. Farther back, the iconic White House graced the landscape. He spotted a helicopter vanishing into the shroud of low-lying clouds.

"I just saw a helicopter. I wonder if that's Martin's. I pray to God he's fine," Eli said to everyone.

"Amen to that," Otto said.

"It's funny," Linda said. "I can't ever seem to remember if Andrew Jackson was a good president or a bad one. I recall that he opposed paper money, yet there are more twenty-dollar bills on this planet than people."

"His is a popular face!" Eli said.

Both vehicles executed a right turn onto Seventeenth Street, generating a substantial spray of water that cascaded over the sidewalk. Thanks to Geronimo's presence, traffic was unusually light, sparing both vehicles from the typical stop-and-go congestion. At Duple Circle, they smoothly transitioned onto Massachusetts Avenue, and another right turn at Thirty-Fourth Street followed. Surprisingly, despite the inclement weather, they maintained a commendable pace, and the tour bus kept up. Inside the cabin, a tranquil atmosphere prevailed, with the only sounds emanating from the raindrops tapping the car and the tires harmoniously humming along the acoustic string of the road. Otto decided to break the silence.

"If you can manage to see through this relentless rain, you'll spot the National Washington Cathedral on the left, although it's important to point out that it's an Episcopal church, not Roman Catholic. Eli, here's an interesting tidbit for you: In the past, the cathedral served as a temporary synagogue for High Holy Day services when the nearby Washington Hebrew Congregation was undergoing renovations. It was deemed more convenient for the faithful than having them travel down to Kesher Israel. The situation marked a significant moment of interfaith cooperation and tolerance. The cathedral prominently displays Gothic influences. Under clearer skies, one would likely marvel at its elegant, pointed arches and graceful flying buttresses. Once inside, the resplendent stained-glass windows create a truly captivating spectacle. Interestingly, the cathedral employs grotesques as part of its rain control system rather than as mere protectors against malevolent forces. However, some audacious soul dared to craft a grotesque in the likeness of Darth Vader. Quite cheeky, wouldn't you say? I'm inclined to view it as nothing short of vandalism. In truth, though, the cathedral has never quite achieved the same level of awe and grandeur as Westminster Abbey, especially as a national shrine."

"We're about halfway," Elrod said. "We'll take Connecticut Avenue up to Jones Bridge Road. After that, it'll just be another minute or so to the hospital entrance."

Glancing into the rear-view mirror, he saw the Imam's bus. Concern etched his face. He tightened his grip on the steering wheel and addressed his passengers, his voice filled with a hint of urgency. "I don't like how close they are behind us. I'm going to pick up a bit of speed to create more distance between our vehicles. The downpour isn't showing any signs of abating. Looks like Geronimo's revenge. I wouldn't want to be outside when the main storm hits."

Minutes earlier, the turbulent chaos in the sky had bounced the helicopter like a ping-pong ball. The pilot was strapped tight in and fully understood how being one with your seat reduced the risk of secondary motion fatigue when sudden jolts separated your rear from the seat. Maintaining his fingers on the controls, he checked his heading and speed. He kept adjusting the headset to ensure clarity amidst the deafening roar of the outside tempest. The patient's condition was precarious, and time was precious. The flight to the hospital was a race against Nature. Inside the cabin, the onboard medics were tending to Martin. The rhythmic hum of the helicopter's engines mixed with the anxious murmurs. The patient's vitals were unstable; every minute counted.

"Medic team, this is the pilot. What's the current status of our patient?"

"Pilot, the patient's pulse is weakening. Blood pressure continues to drop. We're administering medication to help with stabilization. We've got to move."

The pilot intentionally dropped his altitude to avoid a severe turbulence pocket his sensors were picking up. The storm raged around with heavy rain pelting the aircraft and gusts of wind preventing flight in a straight line.

"Medic team, be prepared for some additional turbulence. We're entering a rough patch. Secure yourselves."

The onboard medics quickly responded, ensuring Martin remained secure and that they were strapped in, too. The pilot tightened his control grip and braced for the impending turbulence. Once again, the helicopter lurched in the turbulent air. Rain and wind battered against the glass and metal, making the ride extremely bumpy. He heard the medics check Martin's condition through his headset.

"Medic team, hang tight. ETA, two minutes."

Despite the relentless fury of the outer bands, the aircraft pressed on. Finally, Saint Thérèse came into view, a beacon of hope for this relatively short journey. The helicopter was getting ready to land in the torrents of rain.

"Tower, this is Flight Alpha-Bravo, requesting permission to initiate landing procedures. We have a critical patient on board requiring immediate attention. Over."

"Flight Alpha-Bravo, this is Saint Thérèse. You're cleared for landing. Proceed with caution and follow storm-weather landing protocols. Emergency medical personnel are standing by for your arrival. Wishing the patient a swift recovery. Over and out."

The skilled pilot landed the helicopter without incident, and the rotator blades quickly wound down. In the chaotic weather, a hospital team rushed forward. Some held umbrellas in a vain attempt to shield the patient from the pouring rain. The medics, seasoned in dealing with extreme conditions, swiftly but carefully coordinated their actions. They ensured the patient's stretcher remained secure and protected even as the elements raged around them. With focused determination, they transferred the patient from the helicopter's care to a gurney. The medics exhibited remarkable teamwork and adaptability. They used their experience to navigate the slippery helipad without mishap, securing Martin's safety as they moved quickly toward the hospital entrance. The wind continued to howl, and the rain lashed. The medics' professionalism shone through. They persevered in the face of a pressing gale, ensured the patient's well-being and delivering him to the hospital's shelter with the utmost care. Even with an oxygen mask firmly attached to his face, Martin became unresponsive. The new team entered the hospital doors and rushed toward the waiting O.R.

On the street, Elrod had successfully increased the distance between his vehicle and the tour bus. He peered through the rain-smeared windshield and saw the diffused lights of the traffic signals up ahead. The road was beginning to flood, overwhelmed by the rapidly accumulating water as the drainage system struggled to cope. The tour bus driver, now cognizant of the greater gap between the vehicles, responded by pressing his accelerator to match Elrod's speed.

In all of my life, I've never had to drive in weather as foul as this, the driver thought. *I don't want to lose sight of this guy or risk having other cars get in between us.*

The bus driver noticed Elrod's brake lights and left turn signal and attempted to follow suit at the precise moment his tires hit an expanded patch of standing water. The bus started to hydroplane. The driver was powerless to maneuver. At the intersection of Jones Bridge Road, the traffic light turned red. Elrod continued with his gradual slowing, unaware the bus could not turn.

THE FLAT TIRE

Twenty feet before impact, the bus gained purchase and slowed, but it was still moving enough to slide into the back of the brand-new SUV. The shove propelled Elrod's vehicle, skittering into the intersection.

"What the devil!" Linda said.

Elrod attempted to regain control of the direction, but the SUV started to spin. The center of the hood smashed into a lamppost. Front, side, and overhead airbags deployed and smashed into everyone's face. Elrod felt a crack in his wrist.

After a moment of gasps and muffled exclamations, Elrod asked, "Is anybody hurt?"

"Linda, are you alright?" Otto asked.

"I think I hit my head, but I'm okay," she replied.

"Just a little shaken," Eli said.

"Cardinal, are you okay?" Elrod asked.

"I feel all intact," Otto said. "Hopefully, no one in the tour bus is hurt."

"Is the car still drivable?" Eli asked.

"We don't have an engine in the front, so that's good. Let me go outside and check." He opened the door and was immediately soaked through to the skin. He was examining the front of the vehicle when the shock of the wreck ebbed, and he noticed pain emanating from his wrist. It grew exponentially into a steady, excruciating throb. He squished back into his seat.

"Front's moderately crushed, but repairable. The tire will need to be changed. Eli, perhaps you can help me with that. I think I jammed my wrist. Let me see if it'll start up first." He pushed the start button. Nothing happened. "Oh, great! The sensors know we've been in an accident and won't let us move. Let's see if we can all get on the bus and deal with this later."

Elrod exited the vehicle and sloshed through the rushing water. He shouted over the rain and wind. "It won't start. Can we ride with you? The hospital should be a few miles or so down the road."

"Yes. Yes. Is everyone okay?"

"I think I need to see a doctor about my arm," Elrod said. "I'll bring everyone, one at a time."

Elrod walked back to the vehicle careful to avoid losing his balance. He opened the driver's door and looked at Eli. "Can you pass me the umbrella? I will escort everyone, one at a time, over to the bus. I'll take you first, Rabbi."

Eli handed over the umbrella and then opened his door. The rain was already drenching him before he took his first step. He climbed out and immediately lost his balance, and fell over. With his one good hand on the umbrella, Elrod couldn't catch him. Eli slammed into the ground. Even with all the ambient noise, he heard his femur snap.

"My leg!"

Linda rushed out; the blood on her face washed away to reveal a gash from the crash's impact.

"You're bleeding," Elrod said.

"Never mind that. I'm fine. Let me help you up."

Elrod threw the umbrella to the ground. It shot away like a loosed arrow propelled by the wind. With Linda, he reached down to pick up Eli, who was further weighed down by his soaking clothes.

"Lean on me," Linda said. "I'll help you get to the bus."

"Doctor, go on ahead," Elrod said.

"Never mind me. I'll be fine. Take the Cardinal. I've got the Rabbi."

Using Linda as a crutch, Eli began walking to the bus. Two men rushed out to grab them. Another man came out of the bus and went to help Elrod and Otto.

"Cardinal, your eye is bruised," Elrod said.

"It's fine. Probably just from the airbag. Those things really do come at you in a flash."

"Let me help," the man from the bus said. He was tall and muscular. He reached for Otto.

With everyone onboard, the door to the bus closed.

"We should see a sign for the South Gate entrance just ahead. Take it slowly," Elrod said.

The tour bus rolled into the hospital campus, and the driver saw the sign for the Emergency Room pointing to turn right onto Lisie Road South. They could see the onramp to the emergency entrance the second they made the turn. Linda was the first off, followed by Otto. Two of Imam Martin's men carried Eli. Ibrahim held onto Elrod and escorted him off. The remaining men followed, with the driver staying behind.

"I will find a place to park and then return once the rain has let up."

Back on Connecticut Avenue, Walks the Sky was in his

pickup truck and approaching the intersection with Jones Bridge Road.

"Looks like there's been an accident," Sequoia said.

"It's a new car too. It still has its temporary tags," Walks the Sky said. "Looks electric. Those things are crazy expensive. With off-the-lot depreciation, that driver isn't going to be a happy camper."

"I think that might be the Cardinal's SUV. He got into one just like that."

The pickup turned left. Sequoia got a better look at the SUV.

"Front end's smushed – flat tire," Sequoia said. "Pull over? I'm pretty sure it's his. I want to check and see if anyone's still in there."

"You'll get drenched."

"I won't melt."

"Be careful getting out. I don't need you slipping."

Sequoia got out of the pickup and scooted over to the SUV. She tried the driver's door handle; it was unlocked. She peered inside. It was empty, and there didn't seem to be any personal property left inside. An employee badge in the center console caught her eye. Picking it up, she recognized Elrod's picture. She then placed it back in the console. Soaked to the skin she pushed the door closed and returned to her pickup. She climbed into the cabin, pulled the door closed, and yelped.

"What's wrong?" Walks the Sky asked.

"I've caught my leg in the door."

"Are you okay?"

THE FLAT TIRE

"I think so." Looking down, she said, "It's bleeding. I may have given myself a small cut."

"We can go to the E.R. at the hospital. Put your seatbelt back on. I'll have us there in a jiffy," Walks the Sky said.

"Once we're in the E.R., I'll call the Cardinal and let him know where we are."

"Do you think you can walk on that leg, or will you need me to get a wheelchair?"

"I should be fine to walk on it. It's not like it's broken or anything. There's the South Gate. The E.R. is just off to the right."

"I'll pull up outside, get you situated with triage, and then park the truck."

Walks the Sky pulled up outside the E.R. entrance and threw the pickup into park. He unbuckled his seat belt and opened his door. The rain began diminishing. He slammed his door shut and scurried to get to Sequoia's door. He looked at the wound.

"Ouch, that's a nasty little gash. I wouldn't be surprised if you need a stitch or three. Let's get you inside. They'll have a warm towel to help you dry off."

He helped Sequoia hobble towards the entrance door, and they entered the waiting area. Looking around, she noticed some familiar faces.

"I wasn't expecting to see you in here," Sequoia said.

"Game, set, and match to Geronimo!" Otto said.

DANIEL

Daniel Rivera holds the esteemed position of Saint Thérèse's Surgical Director of Heart Transplantation and Mechanical Circulatory Support, placing him at the forefront of cutting-edge medical practices. He regards himself as disciplined yet funny. Those working in his department respect him, but don't think he is humorous at all. Everyone calls him "Chief."

A nurse walked into the scrub room. "Good afternoon, Chief. How are we feeling?"

Daniel continued to scour his hands, wrists, and elbows. "You know my oldest, the one who just got his driver's license last week," he said. "He was hurrying home to stay ahead of the storm. He texted and said he'd driven over some debris. He asked me, 'How do you change two flat tires when the trunk only has one spare?' I just told him, 'Ask your mother.'"

Daniel laughed at his own remark. The nurse didn't.

His extensive career encompassed military surgery in the intricate domains of adult cardiac and thoracic surgery. In the journal *JAMA Surgery*, his impact was described as "remarkable." He'd embarked on his medical career with a general surgery internship and residency in the vibrant city of San Diego, honing his skills at the esteemed Naval Medical Center. His dedication and commitment shone brightly during this crucial phase of his training. Further enriching his knowledge and expertise, he embarked on the transformative phase of his education by completing a rigorous residency in cardiothoracic surgery at Vanderbilt. The university's medical center in Nashville stood a stone's throw away from Cardinal LaMacchia's cathedral.

Hailing from the charming town of Cedar Rapids, Iowa, Daniel spent his formative years nurtured by the heartland's values and ethos. His educational journey commenced at the University of California at Davis, where he embarked on his undergraduate studies as part of the esteemed Naval ROTC scholarship program. Demonstrating his commitment to academic excellence, he graduated *cum laude*, setting a solid foundation for his future endeavors.

As his career ascended, his leadership qualities and medical expertise were recognized by his peers. He was elected Vice President of the Medical Staff, a role he fulfilled with utmost dedication and proficiency. Subsequently, he assumed the esteemed position of Medical Staff President. He was responsible for chairing the Executive Committee of the Medical Staff, solidifying his reputation as a medicine and military service leader. After retiring from the military, he secured a position at Saint Thérèse. His exemplary expertise led to his selection as the Cardiothoracic Surgery Specialty Leader. This position underscored his exceptional proficiency in the field. Simultaneously, he assumed the role of Surgical Director, where his leadership and dedication continue to shine.

During his illustrious career, he led an Expeditionary Medical Unit in active war zones, a testament to his courage and commitment to facing adversity. His exceptional contributions garnered him a remarkable array of decorations including the prestigious Legion of Merit, the Meritorious Service Medal, the Navy Commendation Medal, and the Navy Achievement Medal. He held board certifications in General and Thoracic Surgery. His extensive expertise earned him numerous academic appointments, further solidifying his reputation as a leading figure in the medical field.

Marked by his unwavering commitment to service, outstanding leadership, and determination to advance medical knowledge. His accolades and achievements inspired all who had the privilege of working alongside him.

"Nurse, do you know the difference between a surgeon and a commercial pilot?"

"In a literal sense, I do, Chief. But I'm sure that's not the answer you're searching for!" she replied.

"We don't get a mandatory time-out after fourteen hours." He laughed.

"How many hours have you been going this time, Chief?" the cardiac anesthesiologist asked.

"We're at twenty-one, and this next patient sounds like he may be a doozie," he said.

Moments before, the operating room had been a hive of activity as every nook and cranny was cleaned and disinfected. All non-essential equipment was removed, leaving a pristine environment. The sterile processing team worked diligently to ensure every surgical instrument was sterilized to perfection. Autoclaves hummed with steam as they prepared the tools of the trade. The anesthesia team meticulously finished checking the equipment, verifying every parameter. They were ready for go time.

The Surgical Director and his entire team donned sterile gowns and gloves. In the corner of the room was a complex heart-lung machine that stood like a sentinel. Its tubes and catheters would soon be intertwined with Martin's cardiovascular system.

A team of nurses gently transferred Martin from the gurney onto the operating table. Minute adjustments were applied so the table height ensured easy access to his chest, the epicenter.

"We have a left anterior descending artery blockage from the echocardiogram performed en route," Daniel said. "Our monitors indicate there may be a few other issues. How are we doing on the anesthesia?"

"The patient is anesthetized and stable."

"Perfect. Patient's name is Martin. Last name?"

"This is Imam Martin. He's the Muslim leader that doesn't have a last name," the nurse said.

"Right, right. I think I've seen this guy on the evening news. He's quite the humanitarian. Let's make sure he continues to do good work. Is everybody ready?"

"Yes, Chief," the room said in unison.

"I'm making the initial incision down the center of his chest over the breastbone. Okay, that looks to be about ten inches. That'll leave a scar! Okay, next, doctor, can you please put the sternal retractor in place? How are we doing on the vitals? Good. Okay, doc, let's crack this puppy open. Careful. Okay, I can immediately see this isn't right."

"What's wrong? What do you need?"

"Nurse, hand me the thoracic retractor. I'm going to spread the ribs a little wider apart. Ready the cardiopulmonary bypass machine. Doctor, take a look at this. Do you see that scarring? It seems our Martin had a previous bout of cancer. All of the tissue I'm pointing at is from cardiotoxicity."

"Heart damage!" the doctor said.

"You get this from certain types of chemotherapy. It typically takes a few years to end up looking like this. Today was the day of inevitability for Martin. Cardiotoxicity makes it more difficult for the heart to pump blood throughout the body. And this has all built up to his cardiomyopathy. Martin, Martin, Martin. Let's just check the values. Here's the left anterior descending. Yep, that's an issue, a heart muscle condition that makes it harder for your

THE FLAT TIRE

heart to pump blood. He's not a candidate for a ventricular assist device."

"What do you see that prevents us from using an artificial heart, Chief?"

"It all has to do with the specific type of extensive damage. Let's get him on that heart-lung machine and see what donor options we have, if any."

"Martin is O negative. So, that'll open us up to all our donor hearts. What are the dimensions, Chief?" a nurse technician asked.

"Let's go with twelve centimeters in length, eight in width, and a standard six centimeters in thickness."

There was momentary silence.

"I've got a match. Came in around lunchtime. The person was caught up in the incident this morning. Injuries were the result of an indirect impact from the car that plowed through the crowd near the White House. The heart is healthy, and the donor was in their mid-thirties."

"Perfect, perfect, perfect. Get it up here."

The nurse went to the intercom.

"We've got seven minutes," Daniel said. "How are we doing on the stabilization? Good, good. Anyone, why did the heart go to the bakery? No? Because it wanted to get a little filling! I know, I know. Try this: Why did the heart go to the gym? No one? Because it wanted to get a little cardio in its life!"

"That's heartwarming," a nurse said.

"Score one for Nurse Cochiti. Okay, I think we have time for more. Why did the cardiac break up with the spleen? My, my, we have a quiet audience in the theatre today! Because it wanted someone with a little more heart! And, right on cue, our winner has just arrived."

"Chief, should I stop infusing the cold preservation solution to slow the Imam's metabolism?"

"Yes," Daniel said. "Show me the heart." He looked into the open cooler. "The donor heart looks nice. That ice is a bit chilly. It just goes to show these Colemans aren't just for beer! They're multipurpose tools! Nice. That's what we like around here – repurposing. And that's exactly what we're going to do right now. Everybody, it's time to get your game faces on."

The lights in the operating room briefly flickered. Daniel immediately knew that the hospital had switched to its backup generators.

"I want a confirmation from everybody that your machines or monitors are still functioning. Looks like the storm has impacted the power supply, and we're now running on our backups."

He received his confirmations and worked swiftly and methodically to remove Martin's heart and then attach the new heart to Martin's blood vessels. The clock was ticking; every second counted. As the final sutures were put in place, Daniel stepped back, his gloved hands still poised over Martin's chest. The moment of truth had arrived. He signaled to the perfusionist to reduce the support from the heart-lung machine gradually.

The room held its collective breath. The new heart began to beat on its own. A hush fell over the operating room. Everyone listened to the steady rhythm. It was a sound of hope, of life renewed, reverberating around the cold stainless steel of the operating room. The rhythmic beats, a triumphant cadence, and a harmonious sense of joy filled the spirits of all those who had been in the O.R. for the past seven hours.

Daniel stood gazing at Martin's chest's steady rise and fall. He couldn't help but feel a sense of purpose. It was a celebration of human resilience, the remarkable capabilities of medical science, and the unwavering dedication of his surgical team.

In truth, Daniel knew that Martin's work was far from over, and there would be challenges ahead as he recovered. The team had accomplished what it had set out to do, giving Martin a second chance at life. The sound of his new heart beating strongly was a reminder that miracles were not just the stuff of dreams – they happened in the dedicated hands of medical professionals who believed in the extraordinary.

With the heart successfully transplanted and functioning, Daniel had his assistant close Martin's chest with meticulous care, rejoined the breastplate, and secured it with wires. The incision was closed with surgical staples holding the skin and tissues together so the body could start the healing process.

The heart-lung machine was disconnected, and Martin's natural circulation resumed. The anesthesia was gradually reversed, and Martin was wheeled to the recovery area. Martin was carefully observed as he began to wake up from his anesthesia.

"We'll take him down to the cardiac intensive care unit in about thirty minutes," a nurse said.

"I think he has people in the waiting area. Can you let the Chief know he can update them?"

The waiting room was typical for a hospital. It accommodated about fifty chairs – mostly hard plastic on metal frames. There were a few bench-style seats with padding. None of the fabrics matched, and most bore signs of extensive use. In one corner was a soda machine next to a food vending machine that contained mainly chocolate bars and packets of chips. Many of the selections were empty, and the machine exhibited signs of needing to be replenished. Alongside the vending machines was a long white Formica counter. A coffee machine could dispense various types of coffee, including hot chocolate and tea. All of these machines were free to use.

Thirteen people occupied the waiting room, twelve of whom were there for Martin. This included Ibrahim and the six others of Martin's entourage, Cardinal Otto LaMacchia, Doctor Linda Herzog, Sequoia Moytoy, Walks the Sky, and Elrod. The one other person in the waiting was a uniformed Marine. He hadn't spoken, and nobody knew who he was waiting for or how long he had been there.

Martin's entourage was the first to arrive in the waiting room. As none of their party needed to be triaged, they had been shooed out of the E.R. waiting area, which was already quite full with patients waiting to be assessed.

While in the surgical waiting room, the men were approached by a nurse practitioner requesting some

THE FLAT TIRE

information on Imam Martin. Ibrahim became the group's spokesperson. The nurse practitioner said they found Martin's wallet and driver's license in his jacket pocket. She asked Ibrahim to confirm his name, address, and date of birth. Ibrahim said he didn't know Martin's exact address and date of birth but that they both sounded correct. Ibrahim was not directly aware of any next of kin but knew the Imam's fiancée had passed away many years ago.

Ibrahim told the nurse practitioner of Martin's work as a Muslim leader and a great humanitarian. He wanted to know if they were "Treating him right?"

At this point, Ibrahim learned the details of Martin's condition. Martin had suffered a severe cardiac arrest. The surgeon determined his heart had been damaged, and he had been walking around on borrowed time.

"His heart wasn't repairable. We were lucky to find a donor heart, and the Surgical Director of Cardiothoracic Surgery was on call. He's performing the transplant as we speak. He's hopeful Imam Martin will have many healthy years with his new heart. It belonged to a younger person who had died earlier in the day as a result of some type of accident near the White House."

"Do you know who?"

"I'm afraid I don't have that information at the moment. But the doctor will come out after everything is done and will talk to you."

"Do you know how long it will take?"

"These things vary, but it can take a good seven to ten hours. It's obviously a very complicated surgery, and we're all lucky to have our best surgeon perform this operation. He's the perfect person to have on your side in a challenging situation. You can rest assured that he'll do everything humanly possible to make Martin's transplant a success. He's the best there is."

"Thank you, nurse. May Allah be with you."

"If you get hungry, the hospital cafeteria is open twenty-four hours a day. However, there's not a wide selection after 10:00 p.m. There are signs posted to show you the way."

"May I trouble you with one more question? Does the hospital have a prayer room?"

When the others had entered the emergency room, the triage team determined that Eli should be seen first. He was sent for X-rays of his leg. The radiologist determined he had suffered an unstable fracture displacing the bone ends. He would require immediate surgical intervention to ensure the bones healed properly and would need to stay overnight. For seven weeks, his leg would be placed in a cast. Since he couldn't drive back to New Jersey, Linda ultimately offered to drive him in his car with its new front tire.

She drove while he sat with his back against the passenger door and his legs on the rear seat. Linda spent most of the five-hour drive discussing her new book, *If A.I. Doesn't Have an Identity, Why Do You?* He would have listened, but he slept the whole way. Neither of them had ever been married, and they found that they enjoyed each other's company. Eventually, they moved in together but never formally tied the knot. Eli moved on from his *shul* in

Sussex County to become an assistant rabbi at a temple near where Linda lived in Princeton. They ascertained they didn't need to see eye-to-eye theologically as long as they both lived in the present, enjoying the now. They never married; she never changed her last name. She remained steadfast, "Even if we were married, why would I give up my identity."

Otto was the last to be seen, even though he was the first among the injured to arrive in the waiting area. Otto's diagnosis was bruising around his right eye and a slight bruise to his right collar bone caused by the restraining system. The seatbelt had performed well to keep him securely in place, but his momentum when the SUV suddenly stopped was enough to cause some minor blood vessels in his scalp to rupture. He remembered feeling his heart race from the impact and feeling a sensation of trembling in his hands and knees. When he placed his hand by his eye, he felt the swelling.

The triage nurse told him, "Give it a few days. The swelling will go down. You can place some ice on it if you'd like. If you feel any discomfort, you may take Ibuprofen. I'll give you a prescription, but depending on your medical insurance, it's probably cheaper to just get it over the counter. I'll give eight hundred milligrams now."

"What a pleasant disposition you have. May the Lord bless you."

Otto would go on to have a successful career as a cardinal, leveraging his network to influence change. Before too long he obtained an audience with the Pope, where he tried to solicit change. After the Pope's passing, Otto lobbied to become the next Pope. That ambition ultimately remained unfilled.

About thirty minutes after Otto sat down in the waiting area, Sequoia and Walks the Sky came in.

"What's the prognosis," Walks the Sky asked.

"They gave me two stitches and told me to take a pain reliever if needed. The stitches will dissolve within a week or two, so I won't need to return. My leg feels fine at the moment. Any news on Martin?"

"Yes, Ibrahim filled me in. Apparently, he's receiving a new heart. He's been on the transplant list for a while."

Linda came into the waiting room. "Hello, everybody," she said.

"Are you alright," Sequoia asked.

"Yes, thank you. They said it was more of a graze than a cut. So, they've just put some gauze and bandage on it. They gave me some Tylenol for my headache. Any news on Martin?"

"The Cardinal just told me that according to Ibrahim, Martin is receiving a new heart."

"Seriously?"

"The hospital has a prayer room," Ibrahim said. "We've all gone to perform the salah. They have mats. We have all asked Allah, the Mighty, the Lord of the mighty throne, to cure Imam Martin. Perhaps you can go too if you would benefit."

"That's a good idea. While I only met him for the first time today, I feel we are very close," Otto said.

THE FLAT TIRE

"The believers are but brothers," Ibrahim said.

Sequoia, Walks the Sky, and Linda sat down. Silence filled the room.

"May I get you coffee?" Ibrahim said. "They have a machine over here."

Linda and Sequoia looked around at the vending and coffee machines and saw some water. Ibrahim brought back three bottles. They all said their thank yous, and he sat back down.

Striking up a conversation, Linda said, "Bob, is that your real name? Don't you have a Native American name?"

Walks the Sky looked at his wife and then turned to look at Linda, "It's just Bob."

"Many times, it's been asked, 'What's in a name?' Sometimes, the answer is everything, as when the name is Rumpelstiltskin; sometimes, it's nothing, as with the fragrant rose. 'Bob' is a name given to people by outsiders, not by themselves. I'm sure it's just a secular name. Surely, you received a more appropriate name reflective of your strong heritage?"

"Walks the Sky."

"How lovely. Walks the Sky. That's such a strong name. What does it mean?" she asked.

"Nothing."

"From my studies, I know it's normal for a baby to be given a name based on their appearance at birth or how the child might resemble an object. The initial given name invariably becomes a nickname. It is replaced later in life according to a deed or life experience. You must have done something special to have such a name."

Once again, Walks the Sky looked at his wife, who gave a slight nod.

"Okay. I have a habit of seeing the bigger picture. It's as though I can look down from the skies and see everything. My name is associated with uncanny wisdom, the ability to see and do the right things."

"Wow. I love that," Linda said. "Sequoia, I also love your idea about a Redeclaration, but in encouraging critical thinking about life, don't think you might be going about it all wrong?"

"There's a bigger action in play too. Article Five of the Constitution lays out the rules for proposing amendments. Historically, it's always been achieved by a vote in both Houses. But there's a second way that's not been done before. It's called the 'Convention of States.' So far, I have gotten nineteen states to pass a resolution, six more have passed the resolution in one chamber, and I have fifteen others with active legislation. Real changes will be coming soon. Always remember, that which is born overnight dies overnight. That which takes time to build has enduring and lasting power."

Elrod came into the waiting room looking a little weary and tired. His left hand and arm were in a cast.

"It's just a fracture," he said.

"There's water in the machine," Ibrahim said.

"Where's the Cardinal?" Elrod asked.

"He should be back soon. He went to the prayer room."

THE FLAT TIRE

"Any word on Imam Martin?" Elrod asked.

The hours rolled by. Silence generally ruled the room. The Marine continued to sit still, didn't say a word, and didn't try to look around the room. The television monitor on the wall continued to broadcast CNN in silence, and no one was interested in turning it up. From time to time, a map of Geronimo's progress would flash up. The scrolling text used words such as "destruction," "flooding," "evacuation," "climate change," "more on the way," "the long arms of outer bands," and "wreaking havoc." From time to time, someone would get up and get a bottle of water or make a cup of coffee and then ask if anyone else wanted something. A few members of Martin's entourage went off to get something to eat at the cafeteria. They reported back what was on the menu. No one was sufficiently enticed to bother getting out of their seats. Dr. Rivera entered the waiting room when all appeared to be dozing off.

"Who's here for Imam Martin?"

All at once, twelve people stood up.

"Everyone! I've got some good news, but the road ahead will be long," he said. "The Imam suffered a cardiac arrest earlier today. He had a blockage, and his heart had been badly scarred. He must've had cancer sometime in the past, and the chemotherapy he received led to a condition known as cardiotoxicity. It would likely have been one of the anthracycline drugs he'd received. So, it was only a matter of time before he'd have a heart attack. And that time was today. Based on the condition of his heart, the organ was no longer functional, and his overall situation meant that he wasn't a candidate for an artificial heart. I'm only just finding out about it now that there was a terrible incident near the White House this morning. I've been in back-to-back surgeries all day. One of the victims was brought here to our institution. Unfortunately, they were already deceased. We checked the driver's license in their wallet, and it indicated that they were an organ donor. Their heart turned out to be a match for Martin. The donor was wearing a work badge on his belt. His name was Doctor Miller Bolin. I learned that he was a practicing Buddhist, and Bolin means 'An elder brother of the rain.' Miller worked at the NIH as a public health policy advisor and held a Ph.D. from Tulane. We contacted his work this afternoon, and apparently, he had a solid work ethic. He was adored by his co-workers for being highly compassionate. He was a complete rockstar at his job. He helped many people at work and in his personal life. His driver's license unfolded a different story, a certain K. A. Lima. Her name was Kamila Ann Lima."

Linda immediately noticed the name coincidence. A gasp of surprise and wonder escaped her lips and she covered her mouth with both hands. Otto, attuned to Linda's reaction, quickly grasped the uncanny connection. Feeling the urge to regain his seat, he did just that.

"We were able to reach her parents a short while ago. They live in Louisiana and are Southern Baptists. They were aware that their daughter was transgender, but due to religious differences, they hadn't been in contact for several years. We told them she was a registered organ donor, and they were very comfortable with that choice. Her heart was perfect for Martin – size-wise and very healthy. Kamila must have exercised and led an admirable life. From all accounts, Kamila was quite the personality despite leading a complicated lifestyle. Gender, lifestyle, experience, religious, and identity differences notwithstanding, it's a good job that all men are created equal. If you want to grab a beer in the cafeteria to celebrate, I think it's Miller time!"

Only Daniel laughed.

THE END

ACKNOWLEDGMENTS

The name for the character, Walks the Sky, comes from the title character of a novel authored by Ron Habeck. I am grateful for his graciousness in granting permission to use the name.

ABOUT THE AUTHOR

FISH NEALMAN, a distinguished luminary in data-driven business decisions, is renowned for his insightful expertise, shared through a series of technical books. With a global footprint spanning numerous countries, his profound insights enrich his debut fictional trilogy, seamlessly blending imagination and reality. As a seasoned professional, he has collaborated with organizations worldwide, unlocking the untapped potential of data. Through his masterful storytelling, readers are transported to captivating realms, as his keen observations form the cornerstone of his transcendent tale.

www.ingramcontent.com/pod-product-compliance
Lightning Source LLC
LaVergne TN
LVHW091633070526
838199LV00044B/1052